CAPTIVATING CONVERSATIONS

TWENTY TALL TALES

JOHN BUNTING

First published in paperback by
Michael Terence Publishing in 2018
www.mtp.agency

ISBN 9781999836672

Captivating Conversations

Twenty Tall Tales

JOHN BUNTING

Foreword

I hope the stories in this book give you as much fun in the reading as they gave me in the writing. Most of them have found success in international writing competitions.

Half the royalties from the sale of the book will go to the NSPCC, so if you like any of the stories please encourage your friends to buy it. Even if you don't like any of them, please still encourage your friends to buy it because it's all in a good cause (and they might like some of the stories!).

I want to thank Anne, my lovely and patient wife, for all her help and support in making this book happen. Amongst other things, she showed great fortitude reading through many a dire early draft, and helping me identify the foul-smelling 'turkeys' that would never make the grade!

Contents

Take the Gamble

The first time Wendy caught sight of Alan, he was standing a little apart from the other onlookers, shaking his head sadly as she threw up over the daffodils in the Municipal Remembrance Gardens. She lunged at him unsteadily, determined to punch his sanctimonious nose, but was stopped by a handcuff-wielding policeman. The first time Wendy spoke to Alan was four days later, outside the Magistrates' Court where she'd been fined £80 plus costs for being drunk and disorderly. It was to be a conversation that would test them both to the limit.

The dank, February mist hung heavy as Wendy marched angrily down the street, muttering vile curses on the Judge and his family. She heard someone run up behind her and felt a tap on the shoulder. "Excuse me," a young man's voice said hesitantly, "can I speak to you, please?"

Wendy swung round angrily. "Leave me alone, sodding press." Then she saw who it was. "Oh no, not you again." She aimed her umbrella at his groin. "Buggar off!"

Alan swerved to avoid her death-thrust. "Whoa steady, I'm not the press. I want to help you."

"That's what all you bastards say." Wendy wiggled her bottom at him insultingly. "Talk to this."

"I can think of better things to do with it," smirked Alan.

Wendy squared up, teapot fashion. "I might have bloody guessed. That'll cost you a hundred."

"Oh no, I didn't mean… oh dear. I was just trying to get your attention. My name's Alan, and I've been sent to give you spiritual guidance."

"Who by? The bleeding Jehovahs?"

"Goodness me, no; dreadful people. I'm a sort of guardian angel."

"I knew it!" snorted Wendy. "You're a nutter."

"No, I am… no, not a nutter, I mean… Look, let me buy you a cup of coffee, and I'll explain." Alan smiled. "I must say, you have got lovely ears."

"Jeez," spluttered Wendy, "arse *and* ears. You're a perv as well as a nutter." She turned to walk off, but Alan pushed round, blocking her path.

"Sorry," he groaned, "I'm not very good at this am I? One more chance… please!"

Wendy looked at Alan properly for the first time. He was in his early twenties, tall, pale-blue eyed and fair with a kindly face. "All right, I suppose you are quite good looking. You can buy me a double vodka."

"Sorry again," shrugged Alan, "but it's against the rules. How about a full English?"

Wendy's eyes lit up. "Now you're talking."

Ten minutes later, they were sat in 'Rumbling Tums'. Wendy hadn't eaten all day and pitched straight into her fry-up. She knew Alan was watching her and could imagine what he was thinking – that she was probably about twenty-five, but the booze made her look a wan and puffy forty; that her tarty clothes were too tight, her hair too bleached, and her makeup too heavy. She wondered if he had any idea why. Only when she'd cleared her plate and was drinking her coffee did she look up. "OK, pretty perv, what's all this about?"

Alan took a deep breath. "Let me start again. I've been sent to help you find a new path in life; a way out of your troubles. You'll be dead in five years if you carry on drinking like you are doing. You're my first assignment, by the way; I only completed my training a month ago."

There was a long pause. Then Wendy said, "Finished? Good. You are bleeding Jehovahs, aren't you? Or a Latter-Day Whatsit."

"No, as I said before, I'm the real deal."

"The real deal what?"

"Guardian Angel."

Wendy looked at Alan dismissively. "Give it up. You're trying to tell me you're from… up there. That's rubbish."

"Hard to believe, isn't it? But I can prove it." Alan leaned over and whispered in her ear for several seconds.

Wendy sat back hard in her chair and stared at him wide-eyed. "No! I never realised! Oh, my… but that means… well, you know."

"Indeed it does. And I'm impressed."

"By what? My backside? So you keep saying."

Alan laughed. "Touché. By your grasp of the implications."

"I used to be clever," said Wendy sadly. "I got a double first at Oxford."

"Wow, you have fallen a long way since then. These must be tough times."

"You're not kidding."

"Do you want to talk about them?"

"You're the Angel, don't you know already?"

"They don't tell me everything. Do you want to?"

Wendy made a big thing of not wanting to; taking off her coat as slowly as she could, and hanging it carefully over the back of her chair. Then, to waste more time, she sighed noisily, and said, "You haven't got a vape have you?" Alan sat silent, looking at her intently. "Of course not, you're a bloody Angel." She sighed again, resigned to talking. "All right, if I can't tell you who can I? ...There was this woman; she was a senior partner at the law firm I joined after Oxford. Before her, there had only been spotty boys and smelly students. She was beautiful, intelligent, forceful; everything I'd ever dreamt of being. I couldn't resist her advances; didn't want to. I was obsessed with her. But she used me, abused me, and then spat me out. I was destroyed. Shit, I still am." Wendy started to cry, tears dripping onto her empty plate.

Alan passed her his napkin. "You gave up the law?"

"I fell in with a bent card sharp - gambling's a habit a lot of students pick up at Oxford. I was the sexy distraction while he fixed the deck. We drank and cheated our way round the country for a couple of years. Then one day I woke up and he'd gone."

"And what have you been doing since then?"

"There's been nothing else since then." Wendy blew her nose and dabbed her eyes. "I spend my days playing the slot machines and drinking bootleg vodka. I can't face the world any more, it hurts too much."

"So you booze, and swear, and dress like a tart to push people away from you?"

"Jeez, you don't hold back, do you?" sobbed Wendy. "I guess so."

Wendy asked Alan to get her another coffee. She needed time to gather herself, and she could see that he needed a break too; that sitting here, face to face with this broken woman, was hard for him. She smiled through her tears as he brought the coffee back to their table. "Thank you. I'm one hell of a first assignment, aren't I?"

"Drink it up," said Alan, "it's strong and hot." His face lit up. "Hey, like me!"

"You're sweet," laughed Wendy, "I might even get to like you one day."

"I hope so. If you can't get to like your Guardian Angel, you really are messed up."

Wendy took a sip of coffee. "I'm hoping this is the point where you have a word with 'Upstairs', and 'He' makes everything better."

"Sorry, that only happens in the movies." Alan waved his hand at the world around them. "In reality, you have to sort things out for yourself."

"Really? Do you think I haven't tried?"

"Have you spoken to anyone? Asked for their help?"

"The Court made me take counselling last year, but I could tell they didn't care." Wendy shrugged. "Sod them, I stopped going."

"What about friends?"

"They disappeared fast."

"Family, then?"

"My parents have disowned me." Wendy looked down at her cup, as if that was it, but then added quietly, almost as an afterthought, "There's my sister; I haven't spoken to her for years. She's got everything; husband, kids, a good job. She knows what I've become, though, she wouldn't be interested."

"How do you know? Get in touch with her."

Wendy shook her head fiercely. "No. Leave my sister out of this. Drink is the only thing that can help me now."

"That's rubbish. In my experience talking to someone you trust is the best way."

"In your experience!" sneered Wendy. "What experience? You're a bloody trainee."

"Yes, damn it," snapped Alan, "my experience. I was a dropout junkie. My wife and kids walked out on me. I died a week later from a heroin overdose. A deliberate heroin overdose. Don't you *ever* question my experience."

Wendy reached over. "Oh, I'm sorry, I didn't... sorry."

Alan pulled his hands away. "Yes, yes, I'm sorry too; this is about you, not me."

For the next half hour, Wendy talked about the hell she'd fallen into – the alcohol, the shoplifting, and the gambling. And sometimes, when she was desperate for money, the seedy, nameless men. Alan kept encouraging her to look at the positive side of things, to find ways she could help herself, but nothing he said could shake her belief that her life was ruined; that there was no way back. Eventually, they fell silent, and sat staring uneasily at each other; neither sure what to say or do next.

Wendy drank down the cold remains of her coffee. "So, my pretty Angel, what now?"

Alan shook his head. "I don't know. Why don't you tell me more about your sister? Were you close once?"

"When we were younger," Wendy said bitterly. "She's eighteen months the older; the sensible one. She was always there with a shoulder when I needed it. She got me out of a lot of hairy corners when we were teenagers.

And what did I do in return? When I went up to Oxford, I dropped her for the bright lights." Wendy wiped her nose. "I've never forgiven myself. I doubt she's forgiven me."

Alan's eyes flashed. "So I ask you again. Why don't you get in touch with her, and find out?"

"And I've told you to leave my sister out of this!"

"But why, Wendy, why?"

"Because... damn you... don't you see?" She banged her fist on the table angrily. "I'm frightened she'll put the bloody phone down on me! I can't take that gamble."

Alan banged his fist down too, deliberately matching her anger. "Then don't phone her. Fix the deck. Go and see her unannounced. Just walk in, and sit down."

"That's crazy. She'd throw me out."

"So she might, but there's a chance she might not. There's a chance she might still have a shoulder for her little sister and want to help her out of another hairy corner. Remember how she used to do that? How you loved her for it?"

Wendy started to cry again, fear growing. "You bastard."

"But I could be right!" shouted Alan. "It might be your last chance. Take the ga—"

"Fuck you!" screamed Wendy, jumping up and slapping his face. "Don't you dare do this to me!"

Alan didn't flinch. He stood up and jabbed his finger at her. "I will dare, because I'm telling you the truth, and deep down you know it. You're just too frightened to risk it."

Wendy slapped his face again, harder. "Sod you,

fucking Guardian fucking Angel. I wish I'd never met you. I was all right till I did. Now... now you've said these things... fuck you!" She grabbed her coat and ran to the door. As she hauled it open, she heard Alan shout after her, "Take it, Wendy. Take the gamble!"

Wendy ran stumbling down the street, barging and cursing past the shoppers, until she reached the steps of the Methodist church. Stopping to catch her breath, she looked round to make sure Alan hadn't followed and went inside. She leaned against the wall at the back, and stared at the altar cross; letting her mind drift through what had just happened. All the things she had revealed to Alan, and what he had said to try and help her. Above all, that fear he had forced her to confront. Was contacting her sister really her last chance? Dare she take that gamble? What if...

A gentle voice broke her thoughts. "How do you think he got on?"

Wendy looked up at the huge crucifix hanging over the altar. "Not bad. He found it hard, bless him, but that was to be expected. He asked the right questions, and it was obvious he cared. And he was tough when he had to be. He took a gamble himself, though, trying to get me to face up to what might be my last chance. If I don't, well..."

"I agree. I'll have a word. You were very convincing, as usual; they never guess."

"Thank you. Was he a junkie?"

"Yes, a sad case. What's your next step?"

"I'll engineer an 'accidental' meet with him tomorrow, maybe another after that, and eventually let him persuade me to go and see my 'sister'. That way he won't be surprised when I disappear. He fancied me, you know."

"Bits of you, anyway," smiled the voice. "Could he cope with a real assignment?"

"As long as it's not too complex – and he or she isn't too pretty."

"Good. Thank you, as ever. Your work testing out new Guardians is invaluable."

"When can I ascend again? These sessions are tough on me too."

"I know. Hopefully next month. When you've finished with Alan, there's one more I'd like you to check out. Theresa; she's up in Manchester."

Wendy groaned. "Another? All right, if I must. But please not vodka this time, it makes me so sick."

The voice laughed. "I saw."

"Drugs, maybe. Coke is fun."

"Hey, steady on! I can't see the Heavenly Host agreeing to us getting married if you're a junkie. That *would* be a gamble!"

Wendy giggled and wagged her finger at the crucifix. "Gotcha. Only kidding, I'll stick to the vodka." She turned to leave. "Let me know about Theresa."

"I will. See you soon; I can't wait to start our new life together. Love you, Wendy."

"Love you."

Romance By Numbers

"I do love our countryside walks, Ben. These sunflowers are so pretty; look, the yellow matches my dress."

"And my socks. Do you know why they're yellow?"

"Your socks?"

"The sunflowers."

"I've a feeling I'm about to find out."

"These things are important, Vicky. Sunlight is made up of many different wavelengths; the sunflowers absorb them all except one, which they reflect back into our eyes as yellow. It's the same with my socks."

"Wow! You can be *very* boring."

"Can I? I didn't realise. But you still love me don't you?"

"I sometimes wonder why."

"Last Saturday, you said I was your one true love."

"I was drunk."

"You said I was handsome and intelligent."

"I was very drunk."

"So you were. What do you see when you look at the sunflowers?"

"A warm summer's evening—"

"That's because the Jetstream's gone floppy."

"...and a gorgeous red sunset."

"Particulate pollution."

"Stop it! Birds singing and swooping—"

"They're trying to impress potential mates."

"...in the sky above a field of yellow beauty."

"Darwin. Survival of the fittest eliminated the grey flowers millions of years ago."

"Van Gogh cut off his ear to celebrate the glory of sunflowers."

"Van Gogh was mad from the lead in his paint."

"Have you *no* romance?"

"I think so. On our first date, I said you had a Botticellian beauty. You thought that was romantic."

"I said I thought it *sounded* romantic. I had no idea what it meant."

"If I'd just told you that the combination of your regular facial features, well-proportioned body and the pheromones you were emitting gave me a strong desire to give you babies, would you have gone out with me again?"

"Depends how many vodka and tonics you'd bought me."

"It was cheaper to say you were like a Botticelli."

"Bastard. Why did I ever agree to go out with you?"

"It was all set up."

"What was?"

"Our getting together. Katie told me last Christmas. She said she was so fed up with you moping round the house she dragged you down to the pub and arranged for Dan to get me there on the same night. I thought I was going to a discussion about the relevance of quantum dynamics in atomic optics, but it was just to meet you."

"Just!"

"I nearly left when I found out the real reason. But then I realised Katie was buying all the drinks... and... um, that you were quite nice."

"Quite nice! For goodness... I'll never speak to Katie again. Change the subject."

"OK. When I look at the sunflowers I see numbers. All of life, all of everything, can be reduced to numbers. The whole universe can be described in one huge mathematical equation. If I had enough paper and pencils I could write the universe."

"That's very poetic, especially for you."

"Poetry is merely a series of—"

"No! You're so wrong. Fields of sunflowers, birdsong, magical summer sunsets; they're what life is all about, not numbers or floppy Jetstreams. I don't love you because you're a mathematical equation, I love you because you're intelligent, funny and good looking. Don't let that go to your head, by the way."

"You mean I've got good genes, and you want to mate with me to give your offspring the best chance."

"You can be a real backside sometimes."

"So you don't think numbers are romantic?"

"I do not. Here, now, you and me; *this* is romantic. Except when you speak."

"Three point five two is romantic."

"Please, enough with the numbers."

"Three point five two is the specific gravity of diamond. Diamond is the hardest substance known to m—"

"Ben! No, don't touch me, I'm cross with you."

"...or woman. The stone in this ring of gold I've just magically produced from behind your ear is a diamond. It's for you, my love."

"Oh."

"Vicky Anne Hill, will you make me the happiest number in the whole universe, and marry me?"

"Now *that's* romantic. Oh heavens, you're serious. Of course I will, yes. Yes!"

"I had to work out the size of your ring finger from your height and weight."

"It's beautiful. The gold matches my dress."

"And the sunflowers. Gold is classified as a 'noble' metal, and has a specific gravity of - ouch!"

"For goodness sake, shut up and kiss me!"

The Last Voyage of Ferrywoman Katherine Marshall

Katherine's first thought as she stirred from stasis-sleep was, "Made it! Now for a quiet retirement in the desert." Her second thought was, "What the hell is all that noise!" Her third thought was, "Oh bugger, alarm bells!" She gasped as the starship's emergency revival system pressed an oxygen mask hard to her face, then retched violently as it pulled the bio-analysis tube from her throat. Finally, as the stasis-bed lifted her into a sitting position, she vomited through the mask and all over her trousers. Ferrywoman Katherine Marshall was awake.

She dragged off the puke-filled mask and wiped her face with her shirt. "Computer," she screamed above the bedlam, "why all the alarms? Report."

"My mother told me never to talk to strange women."

"What?! Damn it, computer, it's me. Stop being bloody stupid!"

"Only following procedure; hint hint."

Katherine groaned in frustration and eased herself off the bed. Two deep breaths and she started towards the door, only to find herself flat on her nose as her legs refused to cooperate. Cursing loudly, she heaved herself up onto all fours and scrambled on. She entered the Bridge on hands and knees, hauled herself up onto her Captain's chair, and pushed her hand into the DNA Analyser. "Computer, Waking Procedure Calamity; recognise Ferrywoman Marshall, Katherine Anabella, service number five one two, authorisation code Captain Alpha Female Definitely Most Definitely Bloody Female

Alpha."

"Ferrywoman Marshall is recognised."

"About time. Turn off that noise! Thank you. And the flashing lights. Now; report why."

"Report why what, Maam?"

"What! What do you mean why what? Why was every effing alarm on the ship going off? That's why what."

"Maam, twenty-two seconds ago, I detected a large unidentifiable vessel seven million miles from us on a collision course. I altered our course to avoid it, only to note with considerable consternation that one-hundredth of a second later the vessel armed its *very* big guns, and changed its course too. So I initiated your emergency waking procedure and sounded the collision alarm. I then checked our defensive and offensive weapons systems, only to find with equal consternation that both are inoperable. So I sounded the action stations alarm. For reasons I will explain later, but to do with the fact that sixty-three percent of my other systems are down as well, I sounded the general alarm – just so as you'd know we have a number of issues to deal with. I await your instructions."

"...Pardon?"

"Maam, twenty-two—"

"Stop; I get it. When will it reach us?"

"In eight minutes."

"Have you tried all the emergency collision manoeuvres?"

"Yes."

"There's nothing we can do to avoid it?"

"No."

"And it's got very big guns?"

"Maam, it's got very bigger, faster, everythinger than us; and it's coming our way."

"There must be something. You're always bragging you have an IQ of two hundred."

"Nothing."

Katherine sat thinking for a while, then said quietly, "So you're telling me we might be going to die. I must say, this is all very sudden."

"Technically, I won't die, I'll break up into several million pieces. But both your observations are valid."

"Well, it was always a risk of the job I guess." Katherine sniffed at her stinking clothes. "But I certainly don't want to meet my maker looking like this." She walked/crawled over to the shower room, washed herself down, and put on her best uniform. Then she stretched and eased her muscles loose. Feeling better, she went and stood by the computer. "I'm sorry it's ending this way," she sighed. "What is it; fourteen trips together?"

"It is. We've had some laughs, haven't we? Do you remember... no... best not to start that."

"No. As a matter of interest, where are we?"

"I have no idea."

"Huh?"

"Maam, when our ship arrived at where I thought Earth was, it... um... wasn't. Nor were any of the other planets or the sun. The whole bloody solar system had disappeared. I wondered if the

problem might rest with me, so I carried out a wide-ranging systems test. It turned out I was A.OK – apart from the sixty-three percent of me that doesn't work. As a result, I concluded that we had been on course – it was the Earth that hadn't been."

"When was this?"

"Seven thousand four hundred and two Earth years ago. Give or take."

"Seven... and you didn't think to wake me?"

"There didn't seem much point. If I didn't know where Earth was you sure as hell wouldn't, and you'd have blundered round the Bridge getting cross with me and using up valuable and diminishing consumables."

"Blundered rou... Computer, if I may say so, you seem to have developed a rather eccentric way of addressing your Captain."

"Sorry, Maam. All those extra years of background radiation have not treated my linguistic circuits well. The foul expletives are your fault."

"So you've never found Earth?"

"Nope."

"Shit."

"Indeed."

They fell silent; both, in their different ways, contemplating the apparently inevitable. Katherine thought about the life she had chosen as a Ferrywoman. She'd enjoyed it. One month loading; two hundred years in stasis-sleep, only to be woken in extreme emergency; and one month unloading. And then a year off before the return trip. It was during one of those years that she'd fallen in love with the empty hotness of the Central European Desert. "It is, isn't it," she muttered to herself.

"What is what, Maam?"

"Mmm? Oh, I was thinking how ironic it is that my last ferry trip – in fact, the last ever sub-light ferry trip by anyone if they've got that faster-than-light drive to work – proves to be the only one ever lost."

"Irony is... whoa, hang on, Maam. Hang on one little-bitty minute; the unidentifiable vessel has started to slow. On current projections, it should stop one mile off our port bow in... ten seconds. And it's switched off its guns! Yippee, we're not going to die; not yet anyway."

"On screen." The vessel was a mass of white cubes and globes, joined together by an intricate maze of thick, tube-like structures. And it was huge; maybe ten miles in every direction.

"There's an audio message coming through."

"Let's hear it."

"Identify yourself," rasped a deep voice.

"Bloody hell," gasped Katherine, "it's talking in English!"

"Never mind that; identify yourself immediately!"

"I am Ferrywoman Katherine Marshall, Captain of the star-ferry Grinstead. I am on a peaceful mission carrying non-military supplies from the planet Oxted, in the gamma quadrant, to my home planet Earth. I mean you no harm."

"Wait while we interrogate your ship's computer."

"Ouch, that hurts!"

It's OK, computer, let them do it. We need their help."

"You speak the truth. I am Becklespinax the Ninety-Second, Captain of the Saurship Goyocephale Three. I am opening a visual channel; I think you will find what you see will be of interest."

"OMG!"

"What is *that*?"

"A dinosaur."

"Correct."

"Hey, my first alien. What a cracker!"

"I and my kind are the descendants of the First Magyarosaurus Solar Expeditionary Squadron, which had the good fortune to be in transit when that wretched meteor struck Earth, our home planet also, and killed off everysaur. How their deep space radar missed the damn thing I'll never know. Anyway, the Squadron managed to land on an habitable planet in the beta quadrant, and the rest, as you would say, is history. You are in considerable trouble, are you not?"

"You're not kidding."

"We seem to have lost Earth."

"That's because it's disappeared."

"...Continue."

"Yes! I've always wanted you to say that."

"We've no idea where to. We've been monitoring Earth's progress for several million years, and what we do know is that a while back this area of the galaxy drifted into psychedelic space, and lots of star systems simply vanished, including yours."

"What space?"

"These parts of the space/time continuum were

damaged when some mindless idiot tested a faster-than-light drive. The effect on the continuum of the impossible actually happening was similar to that on your brain if you took Lysergic Diethylamide."

"LSD?"

"No shit. Warped space!"

"Your ship entered the psychedelic space when it approached where Earth should have been. You're trapped."

"Are you... trapped?"

No. Our scientists have developed a mobile force field that can keep out psychedelic space by generating an artificial normal space around us."

"Wow; that is genuinely cool and very, very clever. Respect to the dinosaurs."

"It's only a temporary fix. Psychedelic space is unstable and collapsing at an increasing rate. It will shortly fall into a massive black hole. We need to leave soon or we never will. And here's the thing; we've been trying unsuccessfully to rescue you for a while now."

"I don't remember any previous attempts."

"You're stuck in a time loop; each time we meet is like the first for you. That's why I've treated this meeting as a First Contact and interrogated your systems as you would expect me to. But this must be our last attempt."

"What do you suggest?"

"Our scientists have tried every sensible idea they can think of, without success, so as a last resort we're going to try something completely crazy. LSD crazy, hopefully. Computer, what are you carrying in your cargo hold?"

"Nine hundred and eighty-two million genetically identical, butter-basted, oven-ready,

frozen chickens."

"Is that animal, vegetable or mineral?"

"Good question. They contain various disgusting vegetable and mineral additives, and far too much water in my opinion, but on the whole I would say animal."

"Can you release them into space?"

"That's up to my Captain."

"Could we detach the cargo hold, and then blow a hole in it?"

"Yes, but as the man said, you're only supposed to blow the bloody—"

"Enough! And the sudden decompression should blast the hold apart?"

"Confirmed."

"We'll do that, then. Computer, make it so."

"Compliance."

"It will be sufficient."

"And then?"

"And then watch and hope. If our plan works, it will force space/time back into normality, Earth will reappear where it was, and you will wake up safe in its orbit as if none of this had happened… which… err, it won't have."

"And I can retire to the Central Earth Desert. Sounds good to me."

"But if it doesn't work, you will wake up in the middle of a collapsing black hole, which… won't be good. We have two of your minutes left; we must act now."

Katherine took a deep breath. "What are our chances?"

"Better than zero, which is what they will be if we don't do this."

"Fair point. Thank you for putting yourselves at risk for us."

"Here jolly here. You dinosaurs rock. Maybe see you on the other side!"

Katherine pressed an emergency release button, and the cargo hold drifted away from the ferry-ship. At a safe distance, she pressed another button, and the hold blew apart. Out exploded nine hundred and eighty-two million frozen chickens. Immediately, the Saurship bathed them in an orange glow of microwaves, and the chickens thawed. Exposed to the effects of psychedelic space, they started to change colour and shape, and within a few seconds nine hundred and eighty-two million pink flying pigs were grunting and flapping around helplessly. Now a green energy beam fired from the Saurship, and the pink flying pigs were somehow twisted and faded into the very fabric of the space/time continuum, which seemed to shiver as one psychedelic distortion was confronted by another. The third-to-last thing Katherine heard was herself whispering, "Our father..." The second-to-last thing she heard was, *"Goodbye Ferrywoman Katherine Marshall, and good luck."* The last thing she heard was, **"Holy shit, I hope the force is with us. Continue. Hah."**

Katherine's first thought as she stirred from stasis-sleep was...

Fishcakes Every Tuesday

The snow-storm battered and keened through the flimsy porch, and I pulled my threadbare coat close round me in a vain effort to keep warm. Somehow, deep inside me, I knew that the next few minutes would change my life - change everything - for ever. I took a deep breath and knocked on the door. A dim light came on above me, and a twisted face leered through the distorted glass door panel. "I know that face," I thought, "it's... it's... oh bugger!"

I woke up and sat up in the same movement. "Oh bugger!"

"Mmm? Peter, are you all right?" mumbled Jackie, turning over, peering up at me anxiously.

"No," I gasped, "I've had that nightmare again. It's always a red door. It was Simon's face at it this time; I was supposed to phone him last night."

"Heavens; you and your stress dreams. It's all right, you said you'd phone him tonight... Tuesday."

"It's Wednesday."

"Tuesday."

Relief flooded through me. "Of course; we had stir-fry yesterday, so that was Monday. Good, it's Tuesday; fishcakes."

Jackie groaned. "Please, not that again."

"What?"

"You! Identifying the days by what we have for dinner. We eat the same things on the same days every blooming week. Fishcakes every Tuesday, spag bol every Wed—"

I put my hands over my ears. “OK! There’s nothing wrong with a steady routine.”

Jackie eased herself up. “For goodness sake, listen to you. What’s happened to the man I went backpacking with round America for two years? Smoked dope and skinny dipped with at midnight while the children slept on the beach? We didn’t worry about a ‘steady routine’ then. Quite the opposite.”

“That was a long time ago.”

“I know, but it’s how we’ve always lived our life together… until recently.” She paused, and then smiled wistfully, “Are fishcakes every Tuesday really all we’ve got left to look forward to?”

“I’m sorry,” I sighed. “I guess I got old. Life scares me these days. And since I nearly lost you, the only way I can cope is… for us to live… I mean, be safe in a routine.”

Jackie stroked my arm. “There now, darling, I’m sorry too. I know it’s been tough, and I wasn’t getting at you. But I miss those days; the excitement, the not knowing what was going to happen next. Look, I’ve been in remission for five years now, and we’re both in good health; let’s try to do some things differently again while we still can. Just little things to start with; like whatsay we have fishcakes on Fridays?” Jackie giggled. “It’s food for thought, isn’t it?”

“Very droll.” I shook my head. “No! That would mess everything up. I go shopping on Mondays, and then we eat according to the sell-by dates. Chicken first, fishcakes next, and so on.”

Jackie spread her hands. “Do the shopping on another day.”

"I can't do that! Think what the consequences might be."

"Consequences?"

"If I don't go to Sainsbury's on Mondays, some of the other Monday shoppers might think 'I wonder where that distinguished looking gentleman is? The one with the fine head of grey hair—"

"Excuse me? Receding white."

"...I always see? I do hope he's not ill'. And instead of minding their own business like they normally do, they might stop to mention it to someone, and they to someone else."

"So?"

"So before you know it, a lot of people's routines have been changed. That affects their families' routines and that... well, you get the point. Soon, more and more people are caught up in the changes as they go rippling out."

"Peter, what are you talking about; rippling out?"

"The butterfly effect. A butterfly waggling its wings in Wigan causes a car crash in Camden. The ripple effect of me not shopping on Mondays could eventually change countless lives. Only slightly to start with, but the effect will grow and spread as time goes by. That might one day impact on important issues, like... like when we go back to the moon."

"The moon! You're suggesting changing our shopping day would alter the timing of future moon landings?"

"It could. And that in turn could affect how and when we go to the stars. Hey, and that brings changing the whole universe into play. All because you want me to go shopping not on Mondays!"

Jackie got the giggles again. "Let me get this right… if we don't have… fishcakes every Tuesday… we change the… whole universe. For ever?"

I looked up at the ceiling in exasperation. "At last, she's got it."

Jackie could see I was agitated. "All right," she gulped, "if you're going to worry about it this much, we'll say no more. Fishcakes every Tuesday it is." She lay back down. "Now, if that's all sorted I'm going to have another ten minutes."

I closed my eyes and tried to relax. But as I nodded off I couldn't stop myself knocking on the red door again; this time seeing a different, distorted face peering at me. "Oh bugger!"

"What now?!"

"It's Tuesday. I was meant to take Kelly to the station."

"Lord, you were. I'll ring her." Jackie fumbled with her mobile. "It's gone to answerphone; she must have called a taxi. She'll be cross."

"She'll be more than cross," I groaned. "I've changed the course of her day completely. Imagine the ripple effect from that!"

Jackie squeezed my hand. "Try not to fret, darling, you'll make yourself ill."

"But don't you see? It's not only Kelly's day; it's Geoff's too - she'll be bending his ear about us no doubt. And the taxi driver's day; and his family's. Maybe his kids had to walk to school, and… and got run over… or… and as I've said, it goes on spreading; an irresistible tide of changes rippling out through the universe."

Jackie snorted. "So is this a bigger ripple than us

changing our shopping day?"

"Much bigger." I put my head in my hands. "It's a tsunami. We're talking irredeemable disruption of the entire fabric of space and time!"

Jackie sat up again and rested her head on my shoulder. "Oh dear, Peter. Well, you mustn't worry about it. I won't tell if you won't."

I took some slow, deep breaths. "I suppose you're right. There's nothing I can do anyway; what's rippling is rippling. And I agree about not telling anyone; we don't want to cause global panic."

Jackie kissed my cheek. "That's very sensible of you. And anyway, hopefully no one will notice for a couple of billion years."

Calmer now, I looked at her coyly. "So… earlier… when you said you wanted to try something different…"

"Uhuh."

"Well, do you fancy… y'know?"

"No, Peter, I do not! That would be a ripple too far."

I raised my hands in apology. "Only asking. How about a cup of tea, then?"

"Good idea," laughed Jackie. "And while you're getting it, have a think about this: if you've already irredeemably disrupted the entire fabric of space and time, and nothing in the universe will ever be the same again, does it matter if we change our eating habits… maybe, perhaps… just a little bit?"

I sighed in half-resignation. "I suppose I could *try* fishcakes on Fridays."

Coffee with a Twist

It was a bitter, east wind morning, and Jack was glad of the ambrosial warmth of the Caffè Nero. This was his one concession to the 21st century; every Monday morning after Sainsbury's, a vanilla caffe lattè and a chocolate twist pastry. He sat in his usual quiet corner, his shopping bags on guard at his feet, his head in his newspaper. Jack's mind was still sharp, but his body was beginning to feel its age, and he didn't want to cause people any trouble. Little did he know how much trouble someone would cause him in the next hour!

A sudden draft of ice-cold air made him glance up. A young woman had come in and was standing by the door looking round nervously. Jack didn't recognise her, so was confused when she caught sight of him and smiled. He looked down quickly, away from her gaze. But a few minutes later she was standing near him, a cup of coffee in one hand, her shopping in the other. "Excuse me," she said brusquely, "I need to sit here." Jack rattled his newspaper, hoping she would go away, but she didn't. He sighed and, without looking up, gestured to the empty chair opposite him. The woman stepped over his bags and sat down. "Thank you," she said, "and forgive me if that sounded rude. I meant to say 'do you mind if I sit here', but it came out wrong." Jack ignored her, but she persisted. "My name's Paula."

"Jack." Still not looking up.

"What a foul day, isn't it Jack? I saw you earlier in Sainsbury's. You looked terribly sad. Are you all right?"

Reluctantly, Jack folded away his newspaper. It would seem conversation could not be avoided. For the first time, he looked at this woman called Paula. Mid-twenties, he guessed. She wore an elegant, long black coat, still buttoned against the weather. Tall and slim, her curly blond hair played provocatively round her shoulders, framing high cheekbones, large blue eyes, and a full, gentle mouth. She looked pale and world-weary. She was, Jack thought, an astonishingly beautiful woman. "What did you say?"

"I asked if you were all right. You seemed sad."

Jack shrugged. "What's to be happy about?"

"It's Christmas soon."

"Oh, I'm too old for all that. Christmas is for young families."

"You don't have one... a family?"

"Yes, two boys; twins actually. They're middle-aged now, of course, with children... well, married grown-ups... of their own. I hardly speak to them, they're always dashing around so much. I think each is hoping the other will invite me over for Christmas. "

"I'm sure that's not the case," protested Paula. "What are their names?"

"John and Paul. My wife, Rachael, she chose them."

"Ah; after the Beatles, no doubt. I love their music and everything that went with it in those days. They were exciting times, I'm very jealous of you both." Paula giggled. "It must have been 'fab'."

Jack nodded. "Indeed. We were war children; evacuees. Our generation, and the baby boomers that came after us, were going to... we did... change the world. But nowadays people just see us as doddery old fools. We don't fit into your, what do you call it, 'digital' world."

Paula shook her head. "Not everyone thinks that, and not everyone wants to part of that new world. People like Rachael and you can teach us younger ones a lot. By the way, where is she today, Rachael?"

"She... she died a couple of years ago."

Paula paused, and then said hesitantly, "Were you happy together?"

Jack shuffled uneasily. "That's a bit personal, isn't it?"

Paula put her fingers to her mouth in confusion. "Oh, I didn't mean to offend you. It sounds so trite simply saying 'I'm sorry'."

"I suppose so. To answer your question; yes, we were very happy. We were married for over fifty years, and we loved each other very much. I miss her a lot."

Paula's eyes flashed with interest. "Fifty years. I see, That's good... no, what I mean is... you were lucky to have had such a long time together. How did you meet?"

But Jack raised his hand. "Please, I think that's enough about me. Tell me about you."

Paula seemed reluctant to do so. She made a big thing of taking her coat off and hanging it carefully over the back of her chair. Then she sighed, and said, "Like what?"

"Are you local?"

"No, just passing through."

"I thought I hadn't seen you before."

"I may be somewhere else tomorrow. It depends."

"On what?" Paula shrugged and stayed silent. Jack tried another question. "Are you married?"

"Not really."

"What do you mean?"

"OK, not for five years." Paula hesitated, as if not wanting to tell him, but then she took a deep breath, and said haltingly, "His name was David. He said he loved me, but we'd only been married a few months before I realised... I wasn't enough for him. We were trying to sort things out, but... this other woman..." Paula paused, staring sadly at her coffee cup, then said wistfully, "It's all I've ever wanted, to be loved, but people don't have time for commitment these days."

Jack was shocked she should reveal such intimacies to someone she'd only just met. "That *is* worthy of an 'I'm sorry'."

"Thank you," said Paula quietly. She took a sip of coffee and looked away.

Jack could see she wanted to change the subject. "Why did you sit here, with me?"

Paula's eyes flashed again as she turned back to him. "It was the only empty chair."

"No it wasn't."

"As I said, I saw you in Sainsbury's. You looked sad."

"Is that how you choose people to talk to? How sad they look?"

"I try to cheer people up; make them happy. Less sad, anyway. It's how I cope."

"Does it work?"

"Sometimes. Has it helped you?"

"Well, you've certainly brightened up my day," said Jack. He looked around the Caffè; several men, young and old, were staring at Paula. "Other people's too, I think." They laughed, and for the first time since meeting her Jack relaxed. How rare, he thought, for two people born in such very different ages to be able to understand each other, and talk like this. He a tired old man with only his memories to live for; she a beautiful young woman with life and opportunity ahead of her. He wondered if, across the years, they saw in each other a reflection of their own inner loneliness. Whatever, he found himself telling her of the full life he'd shared with Rachael, of the joy their children and grandchildren had brought them, and of the richness of their growing old together. He was flattered by how much interest she showed; laughing as he reminisced about 'beatlemania', and prompting him with questions. It was a long time before he fell silent.

Jack drank down the long-cold remains of his coffee and checked his watch. "Look at the time, I'd better be going. I'm due at the Doctor's in half an hour. It's been lovely talking to you, I hope things work out."

Paula didn't seem to hear him. She sat lost in thought, her face serious, as Jack gathered his shopping bags. Then she took a deep breath, as if a decision made, and looked up at him. "Would you like a second chance... a second time... with Rachael?" There was a tension in her voice that Jack hadn't heard before.

"Of course."

"What would you give to get it?"

"I don't understand."

Paula leant forward, anxious. "Would you sell your soul for it?"

Jack sat down again. "What on earth do you mean?"

"Answer me!" demanded Paula. "Did you love Rachael that much?"

"I… I don't believe I have a soul."

"You're not religious?"

"No. What you see is what you get. There's nothing else."

Paula shivered. "You're *so* wrong. But I must know; if you were religious would you sell your soul for another chance… another time with Rachael?"

"But I'm not."

Paula stared hard at Jack; silent.

Jack felt trapped by her intensity, needing to say something, anything, to appease her. "Ok… um… let me put it this way. I loved Rachael dearly; I've never loved anyone else. And I do so wish I could have had more time with her. Does that help?"

Paula stayed staring.

Jack laughed nervously. "What's the matter?"

Stayed silent.

"Paula, you're frightening me."

Paula sat back slowly, but held her stare. "I was testing you."

"What?"

"Testing your love for Rachael."

"Testing my…" said Jack, angrily. "How dare you. It's none of your business!"

Paula laughed coldly. "But it is. I needed to be sure of your commitment. I would give *anything* to be loved like Rachael was." Her eyes were cold as she reached over, and touched Jack's hand. "Don't worry, this won't hurt." The air seemed to shimmer, the world twist…

…as Jack drank down the long-cold remains of his coffee

and checked his watch. “Look at the time, we’d better be going. The new Beatles LP is out in half an hour. What’s it called?”

“The White Album,” said Paula, watching Jack closely. “How are you feeling?”

“I’m fine, thanks. Just went a bit dizzy for a moment. Working too hard I guess.”

Paula’s eyes flashed as she smiled. “I guess. Anyway, I’ll come with you to the record shop. Where are our own baby Beatles?”

“Over there, playing with the lego. And look at them, they’re not babies any more. I can’t believe they’re two next week. Christmas is going to be really fab this year!” He waved to them. “John, Paul. Come on, time to go.”

“I’ll get them,” said Paula, “you bring the shopping bags.” She stood up and put on the elegant, long black coat he’d bought her that morning.

Jack watched her walk over to the toy area, and help the twins into the double buggy. He grinned as three teenage boys gawped open-mouthed as she leaned over, her curly blond hair playing provocatively round her shoulders. It struck him how strangely teenagers dressed and behaved these days. What did they call themselves – hippies? They were right about one thing, though; Jack never stopped wondering at how astonishingly beautiful Paula was, and how her large blue eyes only had time for him. He was so very much in love with her. He picked up the shopping bags and followed her out into the bitter, east wind morning.

The Landlady's Pyjamas

I'd heard that The Jolly Scrumper was a must amongst Somerset cerevisaphiles, and was keen to try it. My new local was packed all evening, and ten minutes before closing time the strangest thing happened. The man I was talking to raised his hand to shush me and pointed to the bar. "Watch this," he smiled.

The landlady had thrown a towel over the beer taps. The pub went quiet, as if in anticipation, as she shouted, "It's pyjamas time!" and went upstairs. Moments later she returned, wearing nothing but bright red, 1960s-style flannelette pyjamas, of full length and with the trousers tied by a white corded belt. She grinned shyly as, to roars of approval, she rang the bar bell, shouted "Last orders, **if** you please," and carried on serving as if nothing untoward had happened.

My drinking buddy laughed at my confusion. "That's our Tania; she's done that every night since she took over the pub. We've all tried to find out why, but she won't say." He stood up to leave. "It's her little secret."

As I quietened into retirement, I got to know Tania well. She was middle-aged, with no apparent attachments male or female; of gentle nature and wry humour. Of course, I had to ask about the pyjamas, but she just laughed and changed the subject. Speculation forever abounded, the most popular being that it was some sort of sexual fetish. Several of us locals 'of a certain age' found this thought remarkably alluring and regularly threw our hats (and some intriguing suggestions) at Tania. She always smiled kindly, but our earthy passions remained unrequited. And she never told her secret.

One sultry night last summer, I was sitting in my usual corner when Tania came downstairs in her bright red pyjamas and rang the bell. We shouted our response: "Last orders, **if**—" but were silenced by an enormous crash. A table by the door had been upended, and glasses lay shattered on the brickstone floor. Beside it stood an old man staring hard at Tania, his sea-burnt face flushed with heat and beer. Tania stared back at him, shaking her head in confusion. Then, as if in a dream, she stepped out from behind the bar, and walked towards him slowly. Halfway across the room she stopped and gasped in recognition. "It *is* you! Mummy made me promise. She said if I always wore my red pyjamas when I rang the bell, one day you would find me."

Now the old man came forward. "She was right," he whispered. He reached out to Tania, but she brushed his arm away. In one quick movement, she pulled a knife from inside her pyjamas and thrust it deep into his chest. The old man sank to the floor, his fading eyes wide with horror.

Tania knelt beside him, his blood a dark stain on her bright red pyjamas, and stabbed him again and again; her terrible, pent secret revealed at last. "And she made me swear I'd kill you when you did!"

A Good Brandy

"Prime Minister, it's French. Sorry to ring you so late, but I thought you ought to know that the Chinese have landed on Amazonis Planitia."

"What?" mumbled the PM, struggling to sit up in bed. "Ama... where? Is that one of those islands they're disputing with Japan?"

"No Sir, you misunderstand. The Chinese have landed a manned spacecraft on Amazonis Planitia, the third largest desert plain on Mars."

"Mars! Robert, are you drunk? They've only recently managed to land a robot on the moon. They couldn't possibly have got anyone to Mars."

Robert French sighed quietly. He was the PM's Permanent Secretary and knew that James Branding had surprised many with the success of his audacious challenge for the top job. The bluff, forty-year-old Mancunian had moved into No. 10 three weeks ago, after the previous occupier had resigned suddenly, citing 'personal reasons'. French had advised several Prime Ministers, of varying quality, and suspected the next few hours would try his untested new boss. "Sir, if you could come down to the Cabinet Room I'll explain. Oh, and President Ripley wants a conference call about this in fifteen minutes."

"Oh no," groaned the PM, "not Sarah 'The Alien' Ripley, she's all I need. All right, I'll be down in a few minutes. You'd better get the Foreign Secretary here; he knows her much better than I do. He's at the Chancellor's birthday party next door." The PM slammed the phone down. "Bugger."

This woke Cathy, his wife. "Who are you buggering, darling."

"The Americans and the Chinese."

"What, all of them?"

"No, just their leaders."

"Ok, enjoy." A few moments later, she turned to look at the PM. "Isn't it illegal in China?"

The PM grunted and headed for the bathroom.

Seven minutes later he walked into the Cabinet Room. The Foreign Secretary was already there. Stephen Marshall was twenty years older than the PM and had spent time as the UK's Ambassador to both Washington and Moscow. His air of Oxford insouciance hid a fine mind; it was said he knew 'everything about most things and most things about everything'. The PM relied on him a lot, and not just on foreign matters. "Hello, Stephen," said the PM, "sorry to drag you away from the party." He turned to French. "Robert, in words of one syllable if you please, it's very late... early... something."

"Sir, fifteen minutes ago, the Chinese Xinhua News Agency issued a statement saying that two hours previously three Chinese astronauts had made a successful landing on Ama... um, on Mars."

"It's been confirmed by the US," added the Foreign Secretary. "NASA took a peek through the Hubble telescope, and there they were planting the Chinese flag."

"The Yanks must be really hacked off," said the PM. "Are we sure about this? Maybe the Chinese painted their flag on the Hubble's lens when the Yanks were asleep." The three men laughed as the phone on the table rang."Prime Minister," said the No.10 operator, "it's the US President. She's ready for the conference call."

"Yes, put her through," replied the PM, gesturing to the others to sit round the table.

"Good evening, Ms President. I'm on the loudspeaker, and I have with me Stephen Marshall, my Foreign Secretary, and Robert French, my Permanent Secretary."

"Good evening, Gentlemen," said the President in her soft, Southern drawl. "I guess you know why I'm calling. For three months now, we've been listening in to the Chinese sending electronic guidance instructions to the spacecraft, but it wasn't until it landed that we realised there were any goddam people on board. We think they must have been talking to them on an ultra-high frequency we weren't monitoring."

'I see, so it's for real then,' said the PM. "Three months; how did they get there so quickly?"

"We've no idea. Possibly an Ion Drive. It's a goddam disaster anyway."

"Why's that Ms President?" asked the Foreign Secretary. "Surely exploring space is good for everyone; 'boldly going' and all that."

The President snorted. "You must be joking. If the Chinese can get people to Mars this quickly they can get them to anywhere in the solar system. Soon there will be Chinese flags popping up all over the goddam sky, and before you know it they'll be *numero uno* down here prestige-wise. Nobody will take any notice of what we say anymore; it'll be the end of the US as a world leader."

"It must be costing them a fortune," ventured the PM.

"Of course," said the President, "but a lot of places out there are rich in the rare minerals needed by our high tech industries. Once they start mining that stuff and bringing it back in quantity... goddamit!"

"What are you going to do, Ms President?"

"James, we've thought about this a lot in the last couple of hours. We're going to have to do something big; big enough to get the world's attention and respect back on us for the next five years, while we build our own Ion Drive. We're unanimous; we're going to have to invade somewhere."

The PM looked at the Foreign Secretary and grimaced. "Ms President, I appreciate you giving us the early heads up, but it's a bit hairy, isn't it. If you'll forgive me for saying so, the US doesn't have a very good track record for that sort of thing."

"I know," replied the President, "but our minds are made up. We must show everyone we're still the boss, and invading somewhere is the best way to do it. Caesar did it all the time."

The Foreign Secretary spoke up. "It might be a tad difficult for us to support you this time, Ms President. A 'US lackey' and all that sort of thing. I'll have to take soundings."

"Yea, well... look," sighed the President, "it needs to be somewhere that can put up a good fight, but who we know we can beat without too many casualties. So not Russia or China; or any countries those two have a real interest in supporting, like Ukraine and North Korea. And not in the Middle East again, there's too much goddam religious baggage."

"That narrows it down a lot," said the PM. "who's left,

Panama?" His two colleagues smiled, but the PM's irony was lost on the President.

There was a pause before she answered. "James, I'm afraid there's only one country that fits the bill, and that's why I'm calling you. We're gonna have to invade the UK."

The PM laughed nervously. "I'm sorry, Ms President, I thought for a moment there you said you were going to have to invade the UK!"

"I did. I'm really sorry, but you're our best option. You'll resist us I know, but you don't have a death wish like some places."

The PM pressed the mute button. "Robert, get the Defence Secretary out of next door. Now!" French left the Cabinet Room at a run.

The PM tried to gain some time. "Ms President, I can't believe this. We're your oldest ally. We've been through thick and thin with you for a hundred years! What about... I don't know... Bugger me, Ms President, are you all crazy?"

The President was adamant. "We've no choice. Frankly, only France and the UK are credible targets, not too weak and not too strong. But the French are the current favourites on Capitol Hill with everything they're doing against terrorism in Africa, so invading them would leave me exposed politically. On the other hand, you Brits are not popular here since BP screwed up the Gulf of Mexico."

The PM was desperate. "But what reason will you give?"

"That's the whole point!" exclaimed the President, "we don't need a reason. Invading you *without* one is the best way to put the goddam hooha up everyone else."

The PM said the only thing left to say. "Bugger me!"

There was a long silence before the President spoke again. "Hey, I know this is difficult for you. It's nothing personal; I like you Brits even if Congress doesn't. I'm going to ring off now, so have a think about what I've said. Give me a call if there's anything else you need to know." The line went dead.

The PM stared at the phone in horror; three weeks in the job and the US was invading! Trying to think, he stood up and walked slowly round the Cabinet Room, studying the portraits of some of the great statesmen who had led the country through crises: Wellington, Lloyd George, and Churchill. All had shown real leadership and fortitude when faced with grave danger. But he wasn't like them, he wasn't a statesman or a warrior; he was a political chancer riding a lucky streak. His portrait was never going to hang with theirs.

He looked over to the Foreign Secretary for help, but Marshall was staring at the ceiling, lost in thought. Just then, Kathy Frank, the Defence Secretary, rushed in. She was an ambitious young star who had supported Branding in his bid for PM on condition she was rewarded. That debt had been paid in the PM's reshuffle last week. "Is it true?" she gasped. "The Yanks are coming? Are they mad?"

"Yes, yes, and undoubtedly," said the PM, "Ripley thinks she's Caesar. Could we stop them?"

The Defence Secretary shook her head. "No way. I was reading up on my brief yesterday. Within a week of us, they've got six nuclear aircraft carriers, four hundred aircraft, and one hundred thousand troops. On our side, the Navy doesn't have any aircraft carriers, most of the

RAF has been scrapped, and as far as I can tell the Army is still packed up in crates somewhere between Portsmouth and Afghanistan." She smiled faintly. "We do have six search and rescue helicopters."

"Six helicopters," muttered the PM. "So we're stuffed."

"I'm afraid so, Prime Minister. We'll put up a decent fight for a few days, perhaps sink something with one of our subs, but after that forget it." She shrugged. "I suppose we could nuke them."

This time it was the PM who shook his head. "I'm not going to nuke the Yanks, Kathy. If I did this country would disappear in ten seconds. What the bugger am I going to do?" He turned to the Foreign Secretary, who was still staring at the ceiling. "I could really do with some help here, Stephen."

"Sorry, Prime Minister, I was thinking about my brother. He's a retired City banker; one of the old 'my word is my bond' school - got out before the younger ones ballsed it all up. He and I had a very interesting chat over a rather good brandy, recently."

"Really," grunted the PM, "is it relevant?"

"I believe it is."

"Do tell then."

"Richard, that's my brother, asked me if I knew how much the invasions of Iraq and Afghanistan had cost the US. I had no idea. He's heard that the number is at least three trillion dollars. That's about two trillion pounds; roughly a trillion pounds for each of Iraq and Afghanistan."

"What's your point?" asked the PM.

"My point is that if we do put up a decent fight, like

Kathy said, and then run a guerrilla campaign through Scotland and the Nordic countries, it could cost the Yanks that much to put us down and keep us in our place for five or six years."

"But surely the Yanks know that," said the Defence Secretary, "why would they be willing to risk it?"

"I imagine because it would cost them ten times that much if the Chinese took their place as the World's Biggest Cheese," replied the PM. "But I still don't see how it helps us."

The Foreign Secretary continued. "We concluded that it would be a lot cheaper for the Americans if, instead of invading everyone who sneezed at them, they just handed over a big pile of money in return for the other side letting them walk in. The other side would agree to keep the payment quiet and toe the line. Simple really when you think about it; saves lives and money."

The Defence Secretary giggled. "You're suggesting we say to the Yanks 'give us a trillion pounds, and we'll let you in without a fight'?"

The Foreign Secretary smiled faintly. "It must be worth a try."

"I need a drink," muttered the PM, and pressed the intercom button. "Robert, come back in would you, and bring a bottle of that excellent brandy you hide from me in your desk." French re-joined them with the brandy and a sheepish grin and poured them all doubles. The PM explained to him what the President said after French had left the room, and what the Foreign Secretary had proposed. "What do you think, Robert?"

French swirled the brandy round his glass thoughtfully. "Well, Sir, I've been in and around high politics for more than thirty years, and I have to tell you I've never heard anything so crazy. It's that crazy it might even fly; you never know with the Americans. Anyway, what's there to lose in asking?"

The PM turned to the Defence Secretary. "Kathy?"

"I like the irony of a banker coming up with an idea that might save the nation *and* make it rich again. And I agree with Robert, there's no downside in asking."

"OK, seeing as there's nothing else we can do." sighed the PM. "But they won't like the idea. I'll have to eyeball them into doing it, and then tell them exactly how to, otherwise they'll screw it all up. But how the buggar do I make this work?" In unison, they each took a swig of brandy and drew their chairs up to the table.

"Make sure your electronic wizardry is switched off," ordered the PM. "I'll take notes, and keep them in my personal safe. There must be no other record of this conversation. OK, for starters, surely they'd never agree a trillion pounds, they'd rather invade us than cough up that much."

"Maybe," said the Foreign Secretary, "but there might be a number that tempted them. Six hundred billion pounds would halve our national debt; get it down to where it was before the banking crisis. We could start by asking for eight hundred billion, and when they play hardball tell them our red line is six hundred billion, say in five annual instalments. The Americans love a red line."

"All right," said the PM, "let's just assume they go for this in principle, and we can agree a price. It's got to look like a real invasion, including to everyone in the UK, otherwise the world will know it's a sham, and that's no good to the Yanks. As Ripley said, they need the world to be frightened of them. But I don't want anyone killed... not on our side anyway."

The Defence Secretary nodded slowly. "What if..."

For the next two hours, the four of them worked through this extraordinary idea. The PM took notes, occasionally crossing bits out, and rewriting them. As they talked, the bottle of brandy slowly emptied. Eventually, they fell silent and sat back. The PM read through his notes, making the occasional amendment. He stood up, and walked round and round the Cabinet Room, hands in pockets, deep in thought. Every so often he shook his head, and muttered, "Bugger me." At one point he stopped in front of the portrait of Lloyd George. "Would you try this?" he asked it. At last, he sat down again and stared silently at the brandy bottle. His colleagues left him to his pondering.

Eventually, he looked up. "If this works you know what it means, don't you? When the Yanks make their payments we can pay down the national debt. Then we can reduce taxes, increase welfare spending, and all that. The voters will love it, and we can tell them it's all down to our economic policies, which succeeded *despite* the huge disruption and cost of the US invasion. We'll be a shoe-in at the next General Election, and probably the one after that. Then who cares; we'll be in the Lords, and the Yanks will have built their Ion Drive and gone home." The PM grinned, a decision made. "As Robert said, what's there to lose? I'm up for this if you will support me." The others nodded. The PM looked hard at his colleagues, as if searching their souls. Then he said, "Right, let's do it." He pressed the intercom button. "Get me the US President please; priority."

The PM poured himself the last of the brandy and drank

it down. He could feel the excitement rising now he knew what he had to do. He smiled nervously at his colleagues round the table, who nodded back encouragingly. Looking up at the great portraits on the wall, he wondered - if he was successful with this no one would know for a hundred years. But one day it would come out, and then, maybe, his portrait...

The phone on the table rang. The PM took a deep breath and picked it up.

His Perfect Mystery

It was a glorious, star-shot summer's night, and the moon was so bright Frank could read his watch by it. He stared out across the bay, as he had done a thousand times before. "It was on a night just like this," he thought, "that—"

"Hey, Grandpa, can you hear me? Are you all right?"

Rhys's rough, half-broken voice stirred Frank from his distant reverie. He took a slow, deep breath, and let the salt-fresh air relax him back to the present. "Mmm? Oh, hello, out for a stroll?"

"Yes. You had me worried there. I was talking to you for ages; I thought you'd… Can I join you?"

"Sure, let me shuffle along."

"Thanks." Rhys sat down on the bench.

"You thought I'd had one of my funny turns? No, I'm fine; I was miles away."

"Sounds interesting," smiled Rhys. "Where?"

"Oh, I was thinking about what I call 'my perfect myst—' Frank checked himself, annoyed he'd somehow let his innermost thoughts slip out so easily. "No, I mean…" He changed the subject quickly. "Look at that view, Rhys. Have you ever heard the expression: *There are more things in heaven and earth*?"

"I have, it's Hamlet. He's suggesting that human knowledge is limited; that mysteries abound."

"That mysteries abound," whispered Frank into the night. "They sure do."

"And there's that word again, Grandpa; 'mystery'."

Frank shook his head, not rising to it. "Do you like

Shakespeare?"

"Not really. I've read all his stuff, and to be honest I think he's a bit over-rated. I prefer Molière."

"Shakespeare over-rated!" laughed Frank. "Molière! Goodness me; fifteen years old, and you're already older and wiser than the rest of us. How the heck do you do it?"

"I don't know, I just can. My friends and teachers all call me 'Obi-wan'. I used to wonder if they thought I was a bit weird, but they seem fine with it." Rhys gestured across the bay. "What were you looking at?"

"The lights. They mean a lot to me. D'you see how they twist and climb up the hill; it's like they're searching for something."

"Dad says you always sit on this bench when you come back here. He can remember you doing it when he was a boy."

"That's right." Frank picked at a fingernail thoughtfully. "Has he told you why?"

Rhys shuffled uncomfortably. "He says it was where you met his mum."

"Met her and lost her. Sophie, my perfect mystery."

"Ha, *she's* your mystery. What happened?"

But Frank still didn't want to be drawn. "I'm sorry, Rhys," he said slowly, "I'm afraid I can't say. I find it too difficult to talk about; I always have."

Rhys looked up and smiled at him. "You're wrong, Grandpa, you find it very easy to talk to me about it."

And suddenly Frank found it was. "Why yes. I was eighteen when I met her. I was here on holiday with my parents. I went for a walk one night, one much like this, and there she was, sitting on this very bench. We got talking, and I fell in love with her in ten seconds. She had a wonderful, poetic way about her; when I asked her where she came from, she waved across the bay, and said, *'One of those lights near the top of the hill'*. I've never forgotten that." Frank winked at Rhys. "Nor the blue hot pants and yellow tank top she was wearing."

"Wow, go Grandpa!"

"We were married six months later, and your Dad was born a year after that." Frank paused, and then said quietly, "She would have been... was... your Nanny."

"Yes." Rhys shuffled again. "What did you mean when you said you lost her here?"

"Well... when your Dad was about three we came back on holiday. Sophie was going to have another baby soon; I'd never seen her so happy. We were sitting here one evening when your Dad started getting ratchety, so I said I'd take him back to our hotel. Sophie decided to sit for a while longer." Frank sighed. "I never saw her again."

"How horrible. Do you know what happened to her?"

"No. The police and coastguard checked around, but they found nothing. They said she'd probably overbalanced, fallen over the cliff edge, and been carried away by the tide. But I never believed it; still don't."

"Why not?"

"Because our hotel was that way," said Frank vehemently, thumbing behind them. "She didn't need to go anywhere near the edge. She was too smart to put herself into such a dangerous situation, especially with the baby. Whatever happened to Sophie, it wasn't that."

They sat silent for a while. Then Frank eased himself

into a different position, and said, "Forgive me, I don't know what made me go on like that. That's enough of Sophie; tell me how you're getting on at your new school."

"No," smiled Rhys, "you tell me more about what Sophie was like."

"Ah, she was astonishing! Beautiful, intelligent, witty; how long a list do you want? But that wasn't the half of it. She was... full of wisdom. She always seemed to know what was best for us all. And there was a sparkle in her eye, like she was amused by the world. My mother reckoned she'd been sprinkled with gipsy stardust when she was born."

"What a lovely expression."

"Isn't it. Everyone fell in love with her; men and women. She only had to smile at them, and they'd do whatever she asked. I used to have to fight them off - sometimes literally!" Frank leaned over and tapped Rhys's hand. "You remind me of her."

"Me? How?"

"It's like... like you're an echo of her."

"We're all echoes of our past, Grandpa."

"We are, but she's particularly strong in you. You have her sparkle... and her looks."

"I don't think an echo would have a spot on the end of its nose."

Frank grinned. "And her wit. You laugh like her too... at least, you did until your voice broke. These days you sound more like a duck."

Rhys giggled. "They say a duck's quack doesn't echo." He hesitated, then said, "Sophie, I mean Nanny, sounds very special. I wish I'd met her."

"So do I. You'd have got on well together."

"It's weird, Grandpa, even across all these years I reckon I understand her. In fact, I think I'm a bit like her." Rhys glanced at Frank shyly. "I've never told anyone before, but often I feel as if the rest of the world thinks more slowly than I do."

"I've noticed that."

"And people seem happy to do whatever I ask - it's as if deep down they believe I know what's best for them."

"Really? There we are then; another echo. I guess it's in your genes… whatever *it* is."

"Maybe." Rhys pulled his jacket closer round him. "Have you kept in touch with Sophie's family?"

Frank shrugged. "I never met them; not even at our wedding. Sophie said they'd gone away before she and I got together, but she would never say where."

"Never?" repeated Rhys sharply. "That's strange."

"I suppose they moved around a lot. Perhaps they were gipsies like my mum said. Anyway, there's my mystery; where did she come from, and where did she go, my beautiful, perfect Sophie."

They sat quiet again. Eventually, Rhys said thoughtfully, "All very intriguing."

Frank nodded. "I still hope that one day she'll come back to this bench, and sit down beside me as if nothing has happened." Frank wiped away a tear with his thumb. "Silly, but an old man can dream."

Rhys put his hand on Frank's arm and squeezed it gently. "It's not silly, Grandpa. And they say miracles do happen."

"Well it had better be soon." Frank put his hand over Rhys's. "You've told me your secret, so I'll tell you mine. My 'funny turns', as you call them, are getting a lot worse. He looked away and sighed deeply. "If only I could find out what happened to Sophie. It would bring me peace before…" His voice trailed away into silence.

Out of the side of his eye, Frank could see that Rhys had assumed what people called his 'Rodin Pose' - leaning forward, eyes half-closed, with his fingers raised to his chin - thinking through what they had been talking about. Rhys was the smartest person Frank knew, by far, but surely even he couldn't…

A breeze blew up and stirred Rhys's hair. "I'm getting cold," he said, turning up his jacket collar. "I think I'll head back to the hotel."

"Oh. Oh, all right," said Frank, disappointed their special moment had gone.

"They've agreed to let me fix their wifi. I need to do some channel bonding in the gigahertz width band range, in order to increase—"

"Enough!"

"Sorry, Grandpa. Are you coming?"

"I'll sit for a while longer."

"OK. Don't you go cold. Are you sure you can remember the way on your own?"

Frank tried to play-punch him. "And don't you get *too* clever, I'm not senile yet. Now clear off!"

Rhys laughed and strolled away. But after a few steps, he stopped; frozen in his tracks. Slowly, almost absent-mindedly, he turned round, and looked out across the bay; a finger raised as if to hold a thought. "I wonder?" Frank heard him mutter. "Yes, of course, that's it! She said it herself. *There's* the clue. And another echo. It would explain why she… and I… my goodness!"

A thrill ran through Frank as he saw Rhys hurrying back to the bench. "What is it?"

"Grandpa, in a minute put your hand in front of you like this, to block out the glare from the coast road over there. Then look up at the lights near the top of the hill, and squint."

"Huh? Squint?" repeated Frank, confused. What do you mean? Whatever for?"

Rhys smiled gently. "Do it for me. And let's talk more later. See you."

When Rhys was out of sight, Frank stood up and walked slowly over to the cliff edge. He peered at the rocks below and wondered for the thousandth time. "Surely not." Remembering what Rhys had told him to do, he put his hand out to hide the glare across the bay and looked up to the top of the hill. The outline of the hill was darker than the night sky, and he could see where the lights and the stars met, as if echoes of each other. He squinted and saw that the hill and the night seemed to merge into one, and that now he couldn't tell which were the lights and which were the stars. And then, at last, Frank knew where she had come from, and where she had gone; his beautiful, perfect, mysterious Sophie.

****

Frank stood staring up at the stars for a long time, but felt no peace. Rather, confusion and doubt grew. Because now he realised there was another, deeper mystery about Sophie; one that perhaps even Rhys couldn't solve. "Why, my darling?" he whispered, "Why? We loved each other so much, why did you leave me?"

Nanny Tweezers

"Nanny, come quickly, something's wrong with the sky!"

"Sorry, Ty, what did you say?" Nanny was cleaning out the stables, while Tyler, who was twelve, played football in her garden with his younger brother, Zac. Mum and Dad were away, trying to recapture their youth in the mud of Glastonbury.

"It's the sky, it's gone all funny; you've got to come and see." Nanny followed him out.

When Zac saw her, he shouted, "Look at the clouds!" It was a hot, blue afternoon. A few cotton woollies drifted gently, but where Zac was pointing they had bunched up into a big clump, like a white football, which was behaving very strangely. First, it moved forwards and backwards, next down and up, then round and round. All very quickly.

"The cloud's wiping away the blue," said Zac, "it looks like a window in the sky." Then he screamed, because it *was* a window in the sky, and behind it was a big brown eye. The eye peered all around as if searching. It looked at the boys - and winked! It looked at Nanny, but this time it didn't wink it opened wide like eyes do on the faces of people when they meet a good friend they haven't seen for a long time.

"Now it's moving away from the window," said Tyler. "I think I can see what it is. It looks like a white horse."

"It can't be," said Nanny.

"How can a horse be up there?" asked Zac.

"Maybe it's good at jumping," said Tyler.

"Horses can't jump as high as the sky!"

"Cows can jump over the moon."

Nanny gasped, "Oh my, you're right. It looks like my old horse, Dove."

"Dove's in heaven, isn't she?"

"I hope so."

Then, whatever it was, it was gone.

They stood for a while, staring at the sky window. Zac, who was frightened by things he didn't understand, crept closer to Nanny. "Was it really Dove?"

She took his hand. "You didn't meet her did you, darling. I don't think it was. You know what it's like when you look at the clouds for a long time, you can see anything you want."

Tyler was at that age where he was *not* going to be frightened. "Perhaps it was an alien," he giggled.

"Perhaps we're all just too hot," said Nanny. "Let's get a cold drink. And we'll wake up Grandpa; he'll know what it was." But as they walked towards the house they heard a loud squeaking noise above them. The sky window was opening.

"Something's coming through," said Tyler. "Two long pole things."

"What are they?" asked Nanny.

"Alien laser guns."

"Pepperoni sticks."

"A mutant chicken, coming to eat us," laughed Tyler, pulling weird faces at Zac.

"Don't do that," said Nanny, "you'll frighten him."

"Is it God?" asked Zac.

"Yes, with cheese straw legs."

"Tyler!"

"Sorry. Hey, I think I know what it is; it's a giant pair of tweezers."

"I said don't..." started Nanny, but then, "you're right again, it is." The shiny metal tweezers came down and stopped in front of her.

"Look out!" Tyler shouted, but it was too late, the tweezers had taken hold of her. Up they quickly carried her, arms and legs wriggling wildly, until she went through the sky window, and disappeared. The window squeaked closed.

The boys looked at each other, not knowing what to do. After what seemed like a lot of seconds but probably wasn't, Zac said, "I'm really scared, Ty, what's happened to Nanny? Where's she gone?"

Tyler put his arm round him. Despite joking him a lot, he always looked after Zac when Mum and Dad weren't with them. "Don't worry," he said, "I'm sure—" but he was interrupted by another loud squeak. "Look, it's OK, she's coming back down." The tweezers lowered Nanny carefully onto the grass and went back up. The brown eye re-appeared and smiled at the boys in that way eyes do when the whole face is smiling. Then the sky window squeaked closed, turned slowly back to blue like it was being spray painted, and the white football broke up into drifting cotton woollies again.

The boys turned to look at Nanny, who was still sitting on the grass. Tyler knelt down beside her. "Nanny, can you hear me? Are you all right?" She didn't say anything, or even move; she just sat there with a great big smile on her face. But there was a strange, serious look in her eyes.

All this squeaking and shouting had woken Grandpa. Zac raced over to him. "Grandpa, the clouds wiped open a window in the sky, and a giant pair of tweezers pulled Nanny up through it."

Grandpa laughed. "Well hello to you too. I knew you'd play a joke on me when I came out."

"No," said Zac, "it's true, a—" but stopped, because Tyler had punched him on the arm.

Tyler said quickly, "We think Nanny's had an accident."

As Grandpa ran over to her, Zac whispered to Tyler, "Why did you stop me telling him what happened?"

"Because he wouldn't believe you. No one will. I think we should tell people we found Nanny like that."

Grandpa could see something was wrong with Nanny. He tried to get her to stand up, but she wouldn't. He tried to get her to say something, but she couldn't. She just sat there with her great big smile and her serious eyes. So he called an ambulance, and she was taken to hospital.

"There's some bruising under her arms," the doctor told Grandpa and the boys, "and at the moment all she will say is "Oh my". Just that, "Oh my". I can't find any injuries to her head, so I think she's fallen over, and the shock has shaken up her brain. She can go home tomorrow, but you must keep a close eye on her, she needs plenty of rest. She should get better eventually."

Nanny did get better, and a couple of months later she was well enough to collect Tyler and Zac from school. As she dropped them off at their home, she slipped Tyler a bit of paper. "Give this to your Dad," she whispered.

When Dad came home and read it he laughed. "It

says, 'Leicester, Saturday, 3.30pm, Grey Mystery, 15 to 1.'"

"What's that?" asked Zac.

"It sounds like a horse racing tip," said Mum. "How weird is that. I wonder if Nanny's brain is still shaken up." But she told Dad to put £5 on the horse – and it won! The next month, Nanny gave Tyler another racing tip, and that horse won. And the next month. Soon, it became a tradition for Nanny to have tea with the boys on the last Friday of every month, and give them the next racing tip. They were never wrong.

The winnings from the racing tips were put to good effect. Nanny asked that they donate one fifth to a charity looking after unwanted horses. Dad bought himself a red Ferrari, and Mum a pink VW Camper. Tyler's and Zac's shares went (much to their annoyance!) into savings accounts for them to use in the future. Dad often asked Nanny where she got the tips from. She always smiled and said, "A flying horse, darling, a flying horse." He didn't understand, but Tyler and Zac knew exactly what she meant. They didn't dare tell, of course; no one would have believed them if they had!

Then, one Friday as Nanny was handing the next racing tip to Tyler, she said quietly, "This is the last one."

"What do you mean?" asked Tyler.

"There'll be no more racing tips."

"Why not?!" shouted a shocked Tyler, Zac, Mum and Dad, all at the same time.

"It's been five years. That was the deal; one fifth and five years."

"Nanny, I don't understand what you're talking

about?" said Tyler, "what deal?"

Nanny shook her head and refused to say any more about it. But as she was leaving she whispered to him, "You and Zac must come and see me tomorrow. I'll explain everything."

So the next evening, Tyler and Zac went to see Nanny. As soon as they sat down in her lounge she said, "First, thank you for never telling anyone about the sky window. Even Grandpa didn't know about it. That was part of the deal... that it was kept secret."

"You keep talking about this deal," said Tyler.

"Yes, let me tell you the whole story. When I went through the sky window I met—" but she was interrupted by a loud squeaking noise outside.

Zac said, "That sounded just like—" but stopped because Tyler had punched him on the arm. Nanny had stood up, and was staring out of the window up at the sky.

"Oh my," she gasped, "Oh my," and hobbled out into the garden. Tyler and Zac looked at each other and followed, just in time to see her being picked up by a giant pair of tweezers. Up they quickly carried her, not wriggling at all this time, up towards a window in the sky; and as she went through it she looked down with a big, happy smile, and waved. The window squeaked closed, and a big brown eye appeared. It winked at Tyler and Zac... and was gone.

This time, Nanny didn't come back.

If It Quacks...

"Wake up! Oh, for goodness..." Sophie shook Eddie's foot under the duvet. "Wake up!"

"Mmm? Darling, it's only 6.am."

"Never mind that, look."

As Eddie stumbled out of bed, little did he know his greatest wish in life was about to come true; although not quite in the way he'd hoped for! He peered into the dawn. "Huh?"

"There's a fire in the churchyard; I think it's a lightning strike. There was a clap of thunder a while back, and another about five minutes later. Didn't they wake you?"

"No, I was dead to the world. The Parish Council meeting, err, finished late."

"Too much single malt with the Vicar afterwards, more like. Come on, we'd better go and see what's happened."

Eddie fumbled and grumbled to himself as he dressed. "More to my life... socks! how can one of you... drunk with the Vicar... no! wrong button... important man like me... where the hell... just want to... idiot, back-to-fr—"

"Are you ready?" A polite enquiry from downstairs.

"...be famous ...ah, come on trousers, you had two last night... all I ask... bloody laces—"

"Eddie!" An instruction, not an enquiry.

Eddie followed Sophie across the village green to the churchyard. The air was clear and cold, and a heavy frost clung to the gravestones. At the far side, in a corner that hadn't been used, a patch of grass was smouldering.

Eddie stamped it out. "There. Can we go now? I'm freezing."

"Not yet." Sophie was poking around nearby. "What do you make of this?"

"Really?" sighed Eddie, but when he saw the large circular indentation in the grass he perked up. "That's odd. It's as if something heavy's sunk in. There's another, no, four more. Look, they go all round the burnt grass. Hang on, a circle of indentations with a burnt area in the middle—"

"Here we go," giggled Sophie, "I know you. Naked sexual rites?"

"In this weather!"

"Human sacrifice?"

"Don't be silly. Do you remember those old TV pictures of the moon landing sites after they'd taken off again? This is like one of them. A bit anyway... except for the grass, of course... and the frost.... and the gravestones..."

"You're suggesting someone's been practising moon landings in our churchyard?!"

"...Perhaps."

"*Me* being silly! This is far more likely to be some of your Counsellor cronies having a booze up round a campfire."

"So what were the two thunder noises?"

"I dread to think. Did you have takeaways last night?"

"Very droll."

"Then explain it."

"It's easy, Sophie. Trump tweeted the other day he

was going to make the moon great again."

"But no-one except you actually believed him! And why practice here, in secret?"

"I don't know, but if it quacks like a duck..." Eddie walked back towards the burnt patch, studying the frosted ground carefully. "Can you see any footprints other than ours?"

There was a pause, and then Sophie said quietly, "Yes I can." She was pointing at two sets; one heading away, and one returning.

"There we are then," said Eddie excitedly, "more quacks."

Sophie shook her head. "Look at them properly; what do you *see*?"

"That's weird; he, or she, was barefoot. No, that can't be right; there's one... seven tiny toes... and an enormous big-toe on either side."

"And each foot is symmetrical. I've never seen the like."

A shock of excitement went through Eddie. "That's because they're not human! Hey, I've made First Contact! I'll be famous at last!"

"Actually, I saw them—"

"I'll be on all the media thingies. I'll be a virus!"

"...first. And I think you mean 'go viral', darling. But you're still missing something."

"I see. The outgoing ones are wider apart than those returning. And deeper."

"And angled forward. Which means?"

"The alien ran out but walked back. Maybe it was late for a meeting with someone." Eddie pulled a weird face at Sophie. "Or something! Or maybe it left an obelisk, with strange symbols on it. Or—"

"Eddie!" Sophie gestured at him to take some deep breaths. "Calm. Let's check around."

They tracked the footprints to behind a gravestone. "Holy…!" gasped Eddie. On the ground was what looked like a large, bright-blue, upturned bucket. It was sagging inwards at the top, and outwards in the middle, as if struggling to support its own weight. "It *is* an alien obelisk!" Eddie touched the side of it. "And it's warm. Are there any strange symbols?"

Sophie studied it closely. "I don't think so, it's… urgh!" She took a step back. "Can you smell it?!"

Eddie took a cautious sniff and gagged. "Jeez," he spluttered, "that's disgusting. What is it?"

"Well, if it was warm and saggy and smelled like that, and it was brown, I'd say it was…"

"…What?"

"Poo."

"Poo! Are you kidding me?!"

"No, I'm not," spluttered Sophie, the absurdity of it all getting to her. "It's an enormous pile of bright-blue poo! Think about it; a passing alien gets caught short, makes an emergency landing… um, poos and—"

"But I've just put my fingers—"

"…takes off again. Eddie, if it quacks… this is alien poo!"

Eddie wiped his hand clean on the grass. "That's disgusting. I can't tell the Vicar that… that…"

By now Sophie was in hysterics. "That what? That his churchyard is an inter-galactic public lavatory!" She started taking iPhone pictures of Eddie standing beside the poo. "This'll put St. Jude's on the world map, and Hello! will pay me a fortune for these pictures."

"But..." Eddie's arms were flapping like a grounded duck. "This isn't how it's supposed to happen!"

"And you, Eddie; imagine the world headlines: *'LITTLE GREEN MAN DOES BIG BLUE POO. Mr Eddie Branding, Parish Counsellor at St. Jude's by the Woods, proudly stands next to the mysterious bright-blue alien poo he discovered in his local churchyard. Is there a message from the stars hidden inside? he asks.'* Ah, my darling, your greatest wish in life has come true at last; you're going to be **so** famous!"

This Damned Heat

I'd watched the silly Breakfast-TV weather-woman lark about in a park fountain, and laughed when she said it was going to be the hottest day on record. Poor thing, how little did she know!

It was a sweltering, mid-June Tuesday, and I'd felt woozy and distant all morning; as if the heat was getting into my head. Everyone seemed irritated by me, angry, and eventually my boss sent me home. As I walked in, I shouted upstairs to Ellie, trying to sound more cheerful than I felt: "Honey, I'm home." There was no reply. "Probably resting," I thought. She was normally such a healthy person, jogging to work every day, but during this heatwave she'd felt tired, and had lost her appetite. "I'm coming up. How are you?"

It was then I heard her scream; an awful, unearthly sound. "You crock of crap!" There was a crash of things being thrown about in the bathroom. "You're so full of shit!"

I was shocked; I'd never even heard her even swear before, let alone act like this. I wondered if she'd just lost it in this damned heat, but when I saw the sheer terror and hatred in her face I knew otherwise. "Darling?" I asked anxiously, "what's the matter?"

"Get away," she snarled, spitting at me, and cringing back against the bath. Her eyes were wild, with pupils dilated. Her body was twisted unnaturally, muscles straining. "You disgust me!" Her fingers shook violently as she stabbed them at me. "You're evil!"

I smiled gently, and held my hands out, trying to soothe her. "It's OK, my love, it's me, Jack."

"No, I hate you!" she screamed. Again, and again, her voice getting fainter and hoarser with the effort, "hate... evil..." Then, without warning, she crumpled, her mouth open rictus-wide. I jumped forward and caught her. Despite the heat, she was shivering. I dragged her into the bedroom, and we lay down. I held her close as her ragged breathing settled slowly, and her body stilled. After a while, she closed her eyes and sighed. "I'm sorry," she whispered. "I don't know what happened. I've never been so frightened."

"There, my darling, it's all right now." I stroked her face. "What upset you so?"

"That's the weird thing. I... maybe it's this damned... oh, Jack, I don't know."

I kissed her forehead. "Whatever, it was bloody scary. I'm taking you to the doctor's."

"OK, but before that I need to re— oh no!" Ellie gasped, pushed me aside, and sat bolt upright; that dreadful look back in her eyes. She peered round the room, panic-stricken, as if in a fearful nightmare. When she saw me, she jumped off the bed. "Not you!" she shrieked, "I told you to leave me alone." She picked up the scissors from her dresser and came at me. "I'll kill you, you evil fucking beast; get out!"

I ran downstairs and dialled 999.

When the ambulance arrived, the paramedics looked worried. "We've had several reports of this type of behaviour down town in the last hour," said the driver, wiping the sweat from her face with her sleeve. "We're not sure yet what it is."

"That's strange," I said, "I've just driven back from there. I didn't see anything."

The driver shrugged. “My guess is it’s a form of mass hysteria. The damned heat is getting worse every day, it’s enough to drive anyone— what the devil!” We all ducked instinctively as a huge clap of thunder shook the air around us. “Where did that come from?” she gasped, “there’s hardly a cloud in the sky. This weather is getting seriously scary.” She took a deep breath to calm herself and put her hand on my arm. “Mr Cope, just to warn you, we’ll probably have to sedate your wife.” As they put on their self-protection jackets, she added, “And this is not going to be pleasant; it might help if you wait here outside.”

Waiting outside didn’t help. I cried as I listened to the bedlam of bangs and crashes, growls and shouts, as Ellie fought. That wasn’t the woman I loved; that was... not human. When the paramedics managed eventually to get her into the ambulance, heavily sedated and strapped down, I could see they were badly shaken. “I’m afraid you can’t come with us,” said the driver, “it’s too dangerous.” She looked at me strangely. “In fact, it would be best if you kept well away from your wife and the hospital for the moment.”

“What do you mean?” I protested. “I’ve got to be with her.”

“Really?” snorted the driver, slamming the ambulance doors angrily, “Well if you must then you’d better get her things together, and follow us. We’re taking her to St Giles.”

By the time I arrived at St. Giles, a stifling blanket of sullen, grey cloud had moved in, and blocked out the sun. The trapped heat and humidity were dizzying, increasing my sense of disorientation. Inside, despite the air conditioning, the air was thick and fetid. Most of the lights had been turned off, and the darkened corridors oozed a sense of foreboding. I stood at the end of Ellie's bed, feeling sick as I watched her twitch and mumble in her drugged sleep. The nurses treating her looked scared, and when the doctor ushered me into her office she was clearly distressed. I waited while she cooled herself with a drink from the water dispenser. Her hands were trembling as she studied Ellie's notes, and I could see her knee jagging under her desk. Eventually, she looked up at me and frowned. "Mr Cope," she said sharply, "has your wife had anything like this before?"

I shook my head nervously. "No."

"Has she been abroad recently? Any history of exotic illnesses or insanity in her family?"

My heart sank. "None. What are you thinking?"

The doctor stood up. "I'm not sure, we'll need to do some more t—" Suddenly, horrifyingly, her neck and head snapped rigid, as if possessed, and her eyes filled with loathing. She hawked deeply and spat huge gobs of thick, yellow-green phlegm onto the floor. "But I'm thinking," she hissed, leaning menacingly over her desk towards me, "that it's probably because she's married to such a revolting piece of shit like you. I mean, there you sit, all f—" The water glass shattered as she squeezed it tight, cutting her badly. She jabbed the bloodied shards at my face. "Get out of here you putrid piece of excrement!" she screamed. "If I ever see you again, I'll rip your bowels out!"

Terrified, I jumped back and out of the office. On the ward, the nurses glared at me in disgust. One of them leaned forward and vomited over my shoes. As I quickened my step, a man in a wheelchair threw the filthy contents of his bedpan over my trousers. An old woman held up a crucifix and started chanting The Lord's Prayer. Halfway through, she flung the crucifix to the floor, and howled, "The vile beast is amongst us! Be gone!" I ran for the exit.

Back at my car, I tried to clean myself up; struggling to make sense of what was happening. Had this damned heat driven the world mad? An eerie noise made me look up at the hospital. At every window, on every floor and staircase, staff and patients were banging on the glass, mouthing and gesturing obscenely at me. Those at the front were being crushed as others behind pressed forward. A picture-window on the top floor shattered, and dozens fell through to their deaths in a howling, writhing waterfall of hate. Shaking and sobbing, I escaped from that desolate place.

As I drove along the High Street, great, black storm clouds began to roll in over the town. I could see the pedestrians looking up at them, cowering, and then pointing at me. A man stepped out in front of my car and urinated. I struck him a dreadful blow, and his shattered body was flung across the road. A bus coming the other way rode up onto the pavement to avoid him, crushing a group of schoolboys under its great wheels before toppling over onto a busy market stall. And at that moment, as I watched yet more die, a shocking thought came. "*Is it me?* Am *I* responsible for Ellie's suffering; for all this madness and death?" Not knowing what else to do, I drove on, seeking out the back streets to avoid people, and trying to ignore the horror that followed me.

Back home, I collapsed exhausted on the kitchen floor; hoping that perhaps here, in this quiet cul-de-sac, others might be free of me. But then a brick smashed through the front window, and I could hear a crowd gathering outside; cursing my name, and keening for my blood like starving wolves. And then I knew; *it **was** me*! I was the cause of all this evil. It was as if this damned heat was melting away my humanity, allowing some ancient demon inside me to leak out and warp the minds of decent people into baying monsters. I pulled myself up, knowing that if I did not leave others would surely die, and fled into the woods behind my house. I stumbled over tree roots and through bushes, tearing my clothes and flesh, until I found a track. I ran until I could go no further or my heart would burst. I sank to the ground and fainted.

****

When I woke, I knew I was different. I felt renewed, invigorated! At last, I was free from the constraints that had held me for so long. My wretched humanity had been ripped aside to reveal something greater, *something glorious!* I could hear people crashing about in the woods searching for me, but I sneered at them. That I had caused so many to suffer and die meant nothing to me; I felt only contempt. I saw that, where I had lain, the grass had burned brown. I put my hand on a bush beside me, and it caught fire. I gestured at a nearby tree, and it started to smoulder. Delighted, I walked on, testing my new-found powers. Soon, all around me was ablaze. But I wanted more, much more. I craved for this wonderful, damned heat to grow hotter and hotter. I yearned to feel the flames on me and they obliged. They tasted my flesh, and I was thrilled; they savoured my bones, and I was exhilarated!

I reached the top of the hill. The firestorm raged about, waiting, and I directed it onto the town. It struck as an explosion, and I laughed as Ellie died; as everyone died. I pointed beyond, and the fire jumped the river and ravaged through a great city. Mighty glass skyscrapers melted like ice candles. I opened my arms wide, and the flames raced on in every direction until I could see their end no longer. And I found myself high above, watching as they spread throughout the land, incinerating the earth, and boiling the rivers back to the coast. There the fire hesitated, gathering, before jumping the oceans and consuming the continents. I rejoiced as the world was laid waste. Then I was back in my body, licking my smouldering skin, and relishing the taste of the filth dripping from me. Where my hair had been, vipers grew, twisting themselves down my belly and groin. My hands and feet were turned claws. I looked up, and the moon and the sun shattered in my gaze. Beyond, a star exploded, and then a million, and then a trillion. I danced with childish pleasure as the universe burned from end to end, and space and time became nothing.

And I raised my arms to Heaven, and commanded the flames to breach its walls, and destroy it utterly. ***And I screamed with joy!***

Old Feelings

***Pain* throbs my bones as I inch to the door.** Standing there are two young women; one tall, one short. Matching smiles and blue overcoats, with tinsel round their collars.

"Hello, George," says Tall, "Happy Christmas to you." Then, somehow, they're in my lounge.

Fear. "Who are you? Get out!"

"Don't *worry*," laughs Short, easing my grumbling joints into the armchair. "Let me put your hearing aid in. We're from a charity called the Fairness Trust, and we've come to help you."

Confusion. "I don't understand." Lesley would have.

"The Government wants us to provide welfare services to the frail and elderly, but at the same time stop you baby boomers becoming benefit busters! We're focusing on those who need the most help, particularly at special times like this."

Bewilderment. "What do you want?"

Tall says, "Goodness, it's *cold* in here, let's put the fire on." She looks at my photos and medals on the mantelpiece. "You must be very proud of how you served your country."

Bitterness. "It's done nothing for me."

"Well we think you deserve better. I'm sure your family does too, do you see them much?"

Sadness. "Lesley's gone. My sons... they send Christmas cards... I think."

Tall sits down beside me. "Is it all right if I ask you some questions? To see what you need. It won't take long."

Apprehension. "What do you mean?"

Short says, "I'll make a nice cup of tea while you two

chat."

But there are so many questions. They seem to go on forever, all jumbling up in my head like pieces of a broken jigsaw. *Anxiety* grips me as I stumble my answers. Lesley used to help me with answers. Tall smiles. "It's all right, don't get *distressed*, this is good."

Short brings the tea and we sit quiet for a while. Then she says, "It will be nice to have your friends visit."

Despair. I wave around my flat; the rising damp, the dripping taps, the broken toilet. "This is a stinkhole. Nobody visits."

"What help does the Council give you?"

Disillusion. "Someone comes in twice a week, but they're no use."

"Why not?"

Shame. "I'm… I'm often not clean. They ignore it."

Short tuts. "I'm sorry, that's not good enough. Maybe your neighbours could help you more?"

Anger. "They don't care. No one cares." Lesley did.

"Oh, dear. Are you *lonely*?"

Lesley's favourite song: *'It'll be lonely this Christmas'*. That I understand.

Short pauses, thinking, and then nods to Tall. Tall smiles again, and says, "George, I'm delighted to say you qualify for our extra Christmas help. It's something that will make things a lot easier for you; we're very excited about it. Would you be interested?"

Trust. They seem friendly; keep saying they want to help.

"Excellent," says Tall, "if you could sign these papers. It's just routine." Pages of meaningless writing, but she guides my hand. "That's great, all sorted. We can start now if you like."

Hope. "Yes please."

Short places a small plastic container beside my teacup. Inside is a large red pill.

A Most Heinous Crime

"Stop!" gasped the Judge, looking up from her smartphone in astonishment. *What* charges?!"

"My Lady," smirked the Prosecutor, Flickr'ing a quick selfie with her, "The prisoner, Mr Victor Conway, is charged with three counts of Anti-SocialMedia Behaviour, as defined under the SocialMedia Enforcement Act."

The Judge glared at Vic. "Mr Conway, these are shocking allegations." She updated her LinkedIn profile with this unusual case. "How do you plead?"

Vic stood straight and held her gaze. "I am not guilty," he replied firmly.

"That remains to be seen," harrumphed the Judge, MySpacing her doubts about Vic's plea, and fingering the black cap in front of her. "Mr Prosecutor, make your case."

The Prosecutor checked his Google+ feed was live and cleared his throat theatrically. "Last Friday, two SocialMedia Police were carrying out their duties in Greynstead Park when they glanced up from their mobiles... um, I should say at this point that they enjoy a special dispensation from the SocialMedia Enforcement Authority so to do... as do we, of course... and spotted the prisoner *not checking his!* An appalled tapping of Tumblr entries rippled round the gallery, as those few 'visiting' the Court in person realised the implications of what had just been said. "When they challenged the prisoner," the Prosecutor continued, "he said he was, and I quote, 'admiring the tulips'."

"Is this true?!" exclaimed the Judge in disbelief.

"Yes," smiled Vic, "they were a beautiful shade of deep red. You should take a look at them sometime. Did you know that red is the colour of love and passion?"

"Outrageous!" blushed the Judge, sending three distressed-faced emojis to her WeChat contacts. She waved at the Prosecutor to continue.

"The prisoner was arrested, and taken to the SocialMedia Remedial Centre, where he was publicly interrogated in the appropriate hectoring manner by SM Enforcement Officers, through CrowdSkype. He admitted eventually that he didn't even *possess* a mobile." The Court fell silent, everyone too dumbfounded to tweet this latest, ghastly revelation. Vic glanced up at Wendy, his estranged wife, sitting alone in a corner of the public gallery. Her tears were dripping onto her touchscreen homepage; not, he knew, for him, but because no one would be her 'Friend'. The Prosecutor pressed his case. "A live YouTube search of the prisoner's flat revealed the terrible extent of his crime - he did not own a computer, a Tablet or any other form of SocialMedia. He is, believe it if you can, *Device free*!"

The Judge's legal wig wobbled angrily. "Well?!"

"It's true, My Lady," nodded Vic. "It is my belief that I have the right not to have a Device; to be private if I so choose. I do not want this continual electronic interrogation of my life."

"But this law requires you to own at least three Devices, and live your life out on SocialMedia for all to see and troll. You can't ignore a law simply because you don't like it!" Vic took a deep breath, and squared his shoulders; **this** was the moment he'd planned for. He turned to address the Court CCTV, knowing that tens of millions would be visiting it, on every type of Device, and that the video of what he was about to say would go viral. He pointed at the camera, and shouted, "You! Stop! I want you... all of you... to stop, and ask yourselves where SocialMedia is driving us!" He paused for effect. "Really think about it. And don't let others tell you what to think; make your own minds up. I've done that, and I don't like the answer. It's giving us alternative facts—"

"—Oh, come on, Mr Conway," interrupted the Judge. "The notion of alternative facts is just fake news."

Vic ignored her. "...and virtual worlds, where nothing is as it seems. It's being done deliberately to lie to us; to control us. And this law is the next step; it's forcing us to give up our right to privacy; to think for ourselves, and keep our own counsel; to have the freedom to be alone, for better or worse. You mustn't—"

The Judge slammed her hand down on her desk, almost knocking the black cap onto the floor. "Enough! How long have you held this deluded and criminal notion?"

"Most of my adult life. Since I started..." here he emphasised, "*to think for myself.*"

"To think for yourself!!" screeched the Judge. "How dare you! You're obviously mad. Mr Prosecutor, have you finished?"

"Yes, that is all. The supporting electronic evidence has been published on every SocialMedia platform; there to be seen and sneered at by everyone. It is, I submit, conclusive. The Prosecutor finished with a flourish. "The prisoner is humiliated, and thus guilty!"

The Judge nodded her agreement and WhatsApp'ed the Court Clerk. "What is the verdict?"

"My Lady; there are approximately ninety-two million

Facebook Likes for guilty… oh… and one for innocent."

"Innocent!"

The flustered Clerk sent an 'Urgent' ViberText to her BessaFriend at CyberHack Inc. "Forgive me, My Lady, I will have the culprit identified and arrested within the next twelve hours. Their punishment will be the same as the prisoner's."

The Judge's eyes flashed. "Good." She stood up and placed the black cap on top of her wig. She posed for the barrage of photos that recorded the moment on Instagram, then turned to Vic. "Mr Conway, you have been found guilty of a most heinous crime, and there is only one punishment. You will be taken from this place, and banished to the SocialMedia-free Island of Barbados. There, you will live out your life barred from all forms of SocialMedia, and without contact with anyone except for those unfortunates incarcerated in that place for the same reason. And may your God have mercy on your soul."

Vic bowed to her, and to the inevitable. "May I make a last request?"

"I suppose so," sighed the Judge, "under this extraordinary circumstance."

Vic took a deep breath. "I wish to write a letter."

"A what?!"

"A private letter. I understand Whistl still occasionally hand deliver ancient, pre-SocialMedia parchments for a fee. I'm sure they would deliver my letter… under the circumstances."

"I will allow it," snorted the Judge, "but more shame on you for aggravating your crime. I will have pen and paper sent to your cell; that's assuming we have any!

Take the prisoner down!"

An hour later, Vic picked up the pen and wrote his letter.

"Tuesday, 14th. My darling Nancy, or should I still call you My Lady! You looked so sexy in your wig I almost...

Our plan only went and worked!! I am being shipped out to Barbados tomorrow and set adrift in a row-boat half a mile off the coast. I expect by then you will have been identified and charged with 'liking' my innocence. I will be waiting for you.

Soon, we will be walking hand-in-hand along an empty, sun-drenched beach, watching the flying fish jump onto our barbeque, and picking fresh bananas and plums. We'll make love under the quiet stars, naked and alone at last, and let this crazy SocialMedia world self-destruct without us. I cannot wait.

With all my heart.

Vic."

Anything and Everything

"Oh look," sighed Alex, "there goes another."

"Mmm? What did you say?"

"And at last the Kraken wakes! My shoulder's gone numb holding you up."

Maddie rubbed her neck gently. "Sorry, darling, I must have dozed off."

"That'll be the three large gins you had at dinner," laughed Alex. They were sitting on the side of an old dinghy, about half a mile off the coast, their feet caressing the warm Caribbean Sea as they watched the shoals of tiny, black fish dart in and out of the smudges of moonlight. "What I said was: 'there goes another'... aircraft... landing." He pointed to the plane whispering its way towards the Island's little airport, its navigation lights flashing across the constellations they had grown to know so well.

"You and your blooming aircraft."

"I don't know how they manage to stop on such a short runway." Alex winced, and held his side, hoping Maddie wouldn't notice in the dark. "Do you remember our first flight here?"

"You ask me that every time we come."

"It was a hell of a journey, though, wasn't it? Twenty hours and three rickety planes."

"You were so nervous," laughed Maddie, "booking a summer holiday so far away. It wasn't the done thing forty years ago."

"I was scared stiff you wouldn't like it."

"So was I. But then we got off the plane, and that

wonderful wall of heat hit us, and we smelt the wild orchids. We fell in love with the Island there and then. And that first evening, as we walked along the beach, watching the sun set out at sea and listening to the nightingales singing... it was like the Island was welcoming us."

Alex nodded. "More than that; like it was telling us we belonged here. The couple we sat with for dinner that first week said the same. They'd been spending their summers here for years; said they could never go anywhere else. It's funny we never saw them again."

A car's musical air-horn blared across the water. "Look," Alex said, "the coast's lit up like Vegas. It's changed so much, hasn't it? The first time we took a dingy out at night, we couldn't see the Island a hundred yards away. Then the bloody thing broke down, and we drifted for hours. We nearly missed our flight home the next morning. Still, it had its compensations; wasn't that the night Sandra was conceived?"

Maddie giggled. "That holiday, anyway. And you've taken a dingy out on our last night ever since; usually the most rickety."

"I've always tried to hire the same one, or something similar. I've had some of my finest moments in those dinghies."

"In your opinion!"

"Indeed. Seriously though, out here on the water at night I've found peace more than anywhere else."

"You threw up over the side last year. That wasn't very peaceful."

"No, that was the goat curry." Alex sucked his teeth and held his side again. "But you know what I mean.

You and me, floating through a million stars—"

"Wow! How much have *you* drunk?"

"...the gentle warmth of the night—"

"You're rambling."

"...the smell of the orchids and the sea. And everywhere the silence. It's how things must have been before... before everything else got in the way. I need to soak it all up; store it for when times get hard. And it was one bottle of wine, by the way."

Maddie smiled gently. "I do love you."

Alex splashed his feet around, as more fish swirled through his toes. "We've not done badly have we? What is it, thirty-two summers here? I'm surprised they haven't re-named the airport toilets after us. You used to joke that England was just somewhere we visited before we came home." He sighed. "It's been hard, though. We've scrimped so much to afford the flights; still do. We rarely go out, and when we do all we ever talk about is our summers here. I suppose it's why we never keep friends for long."

"I've no regrets," said Maddie vehemently. "I love it here. I'd do anything to come back. Every time I do I've felt that wonderful welcome; that drawing me in again. The Island means everything to me."

"Me too. Sandra once asked me why we never brought her here when she was young; why she always had to stay with your Mum. I think it hurt her; still does."

"I know. She's challenged me about it several times recently. She thinks we were selfish, particularly that year we came so soon after she broke her leg. She said she cried for a week, and so did my Mum. I think it's why she never brings the boys to see us. I hadn't realised she felt so strongly."

Alex shrugged. "I'm sorry she feels that way, but it's not our fault. It's the Island that's selfish, not us. We *have* to come back, it makes us. I wish people could understand."

The dinghy bobbed as a breeze caught it, and the moon faded behind a cloud. Alex shivered. "There's a storm coming, I can feel the chill."

Maddie didn't seem to hear him. "My favourite place is the Flower Forest. You walk through that deep jungle, so full of humidity and colour, and then suddenly you come out into that clearing. The sun's blazing, and you can see down along the beach for miles. I could look at that view for ever."

"Wasn't that where the green monkey ran out and pinched your bottom? The waitress at the hotel screamed with laughter when I told her; she said it was part of the male monkey mating ritual. The other guests were in fits."

"I've never been so embarrassed in all my life! The waitress talked of nothing else the whole holiday."

They sat quiet for a long time, feet playing in the water, dreaming their many Island memories. Eventually, Alex said, "It must have been a shock for Sandra, your bad news. And coming so soon after mine. What do you think she's doing?"

"Wondering what the hell to do with us when we get back, I expect."

Alex put his arm round Maddie's shoulder. "Is it hurting a lot?"

"It comes and goes. I think the painkillers are wearing off. What about you?"

"I took some tramadol after dinner."

"On top of all that wine!"

"It doesn't really matter any more, does it?"

The dinghy rocked again, more heavily, and the breeze blew stronger. "I'm going cold too," Maddie said, "I don't want to stay out here much longer." She sighed. "I think it's time to go."

"Are you sure? Can't we stay five more minutes?"

Maddie laid her head on his shoulder. "No, darling, my neck hurts a lot, and I'm very tired. It's time."

Alex looked up, trying to pick out the constellations one more time; but they were hidden by the storm clouds. He looked over to the Island, and murmured, "Thank you." He pulled Maddie close, and kissed her hair, and at the same time pushed the heavy rock off his lap. The rope round their ankles jerked tight, and Maddie gasped as they were pulled off the dingy and under the water. They struggled for a few moments, something inside them fighting to live, but they were old, and they were ill, and the struggle was brief. They sank quickly, and soon they were at peace amongst the bones of all those others who had loved the Island and could not leave.

The ancient dinghy drifted with the tide back towards the coast. There would be other couples. Above, another plane whispered its way towards the airport. On board, a nervous young man held his girl tight and pointed excitedly at the lights below. Their first summer holiday together; how he hoped she would like it here. And the Island felt them coming and reached out to welcome them.

The Generous Genie

There was a blinding flash and a thunderous crash. "Greetings," boomed a deep voice, "I am The Mighty Metjen; friend and confidante of The Golden King Tutankhamun, Protector of His Harem, and Slayer of His enemies. For three thousand years, I have been genie of His Imperial Magic Lamp, and by His glorious power vested in me I grant you two wishes!"

"Wow," gasped Mike, jumping back in fright. "That was quite an entrance." He'd been sorting out his mother's loft and had found the grubby little lamp wrapped in rags inside an old wooden box. He rubbed his eyes to clear them and peered at the genie. "Oh, my goodness, she was right. I never... hang on... *two* wishes?"

"Yes, yes, I know," groaned the genie, "but everyone's cutting back at the moment. First there was austerity, and now with all this Brexit bollo... my apologies, I nearly used some unnecessary language there. Please, who is 'she'?"

But Mike ignored the question. "Can I wish for anything?"

"That depends," shrugged the genie. "I've discontinued some of my more, how shall I put it, 'exotic' wishes. But let us not get ahead of ourselves; do me the honour of telling me whom I am addressing."

"Of course. My name is Mike Braxton."

The genie bowed in welcome. "And what it is you seek, Mike Braxton?"

"Oh, that's easy. First of all, a complete break, and then a fresh start in life. I'm in a bad place; I've lost my job, my car has been repossessed, and last week my old mum died." Mike sighed. "I feel very alone at the moment." He waved round the loft. "This is mum's, by the way."

"Ah, so she's the 'she'. I'm sorry for your loss, your mother was a fine woman."

"That's kind of you, she was. I shall miss her." Mike eased himself down onto an upturned packing case. "She talked about you towards the end. To be honest, I didn't believe… the last few years were difficult for her."

The genie smiled sympathetically. "I understand. She was the last person to use my very considerable services. That is how my lamp finished up here; I asked her to keep it somewhere safe."

"I see. What wishes did—"

"No, Mike, let me stop you there," interrupted the genie, "I cannot, I must not, say. The Guild of Generous Genii is very strict on client confidentiality. It is time now to focus on you." The genie placed a comforting hand on Mike's shoulder. "And fear not; as it happens, I specialise in helping lonely people looking for a fresh start. I should tell you, however, that I'm only qualified to level four, but I'll do the best I can. Try me; wish me your wishes."

Mike scratched his nose. "How about make me a millionaire?"

The genie sucked its teeth. "That's a tough one. It really needs a level six."

"Health and happiness?"

"Nooo. Much too vague."

"You're not a very good genie, are you?" laughed Mike sort of half good-naturedly.

"I'm the only one you've got," harrumphed the genie, assuming the teapot position.

Mike raised his hand in apology. "Fair point; let's keep trying. Can you stop Lara - she's my wife - having a go at me all the time?"

"I could strike her dumb, but surely that's a wasted wish. Why not buy some earplugs?"

"I did; I couldn't hear the television."

"OK, leave her. You want a fresh start."

"No, no, I love her really, I couldn't do that. It's just her way of dealing with the stress we're under." Mike grinned. "And anyway, who would cook my dinners?"

The genie winced. "Harsh."

"I was only joking!"

"Forgive me, I'm a bit naive sometimes. Being a genie, I don't get out all that often." The genie stroked its beard and looked at Mike quizzically. "So... you seek peace and quiet while you get yourself sorted, do you? I can understand that. I must say, it's what I like about living inside my lamp. Nothing but me, a comfy chair, and the Xbox; peace and quiet guaranteed. Tranquillity Base, I call it. The genie suddenly raised a finger to its mouth as it had an idea. "Hey, why don't you and I swop places for a while. You'd really like it in there. It could be your first wish."

"What?" gasped Mike, shocked by the suggestion. "Me become... um... a genie?"

"Yes. An honorary genie, anyway. I'd fix it with the Guild that you didn't have the power to spirit out of the lamp, and grant any wishes."

"But you'd be swopping your lovely lamp for my

nagging wife. It's not really fair on you, is it?"

"I don't mind. It would be good to have some company for a change, and I'll make sure she's well provided for while you're away."

"Huh?"

The genie gestured apologetically. "Only financially, you understand. I'm not suggesting… I mean, all us genii have been… you know…"

"Indeed," laughed Mike. "How long would this be for?"

"Just a short while; say three months. After that, I could swop us back and then… let's see… how about if I set Lara and you up in a beach bar somewhere hot and sunny? That could be your second wish. Yes, the more I think about it that's it. A complete break, like you said, followed by a new life for you both in Barbados. I can see the sign now: **'Drinkin' an' Limin' wit Mikey and L…'** oh… no… but I daresay we can work on that. "Well?" pressed the genie eagerly, "what do you think of it?"

Mike wasn't sure what he thought of it. "It sounds simple enough, but what about things like my meals?"

"No problem; they'll just appear on your table three times a day… like magic." The genie giggled at its own joke.

"But you must get bored sitting there playing computer games month after month."

"Au contraire. I've got Grand Theft Auto, Fifa 18, and lots more."

Mike shook his head. "No, it's not enough. I like watching the sport on the television. I couldn't give that up."

"Hah, that's not a problem either. I've adapted the

Xbox to get all the sports channels. The lamp handle makes an excellent TV aerial."

"It's kind of you, but—"

"And it can get all the porn channels," added the genie quickly. "So, what do you think, shall we go for it? You know it makes sense."

Mike scratched his nose again. "All the porn channels, you say?"

"Yep."

"And all the sports?"

"Uhuh. You'll want for nothing."

Mike went quiet for a while; still scratching; thinking hard about the genie's plan. Then he laughed, a decision made. "All right, if you're sure; it's very generous of you. I would like some time to get my head straight about mum. Those are my two wishes." He waited in anticipation, but nothing happened. "What more do you want me to say? Pretty please, I'm sure they are?" Still nothing. He looked the genie in the eye. "Oh Mighty Metjen of the Imperial Magic Lamp, I command you to swop places with me for three months, and when I return to set Lara and me up in a beach bar in Barbados. Make it so."

The genie stood straight and made a complex flourish of signs with its right hand. Then it gestured to the magic lamp with its left. "Mike Braxton, your wish is my command."

There was a blinding flash and a thunderous crash, and Mike found himself inside the lamp. It was exactly as the genie had said; quiet, an armchair, and an Xbox. He sighed with relief at his change of fortune and sat down contentedly. But moments later a terrifying voice behind him screeched, *"Who the bleedin' 'ell are you?"* Mike jumped up in fright and spun round. There stood the ugliest woman he'd ever seen. Short, hugely fat, with long, greasy white hair that didn't quite hide the multitude of weeping warts on her ruined face. "Ah, I see," snorted the hag, "the old buggar's finally found someone stupid enough to swop places wiv 'im 'as 'e? Did 'e pretend to be a h'ancient Egyptian?" Mike nodded dumbly. "I thought so. Well 'e's a lying git, 'is name's 'arry 'epplewhite, and 'e's from 'ull. 'e's been trapped in this soddin' lamp with me for forty years." Mike stared aghast as the horror heaved herself over to him, and thrust her monstrous breasts into his stomach. He felt sick at the smell of her. "So, what's 'e left me wiv?" she wheezed, leering at Mike up and down. "Yum, fresh young meat. And strong too; what a generous bleeder 'e is." She farted loudly and fetidly. "Come on, then, there's no poncin' around in 'ere. There's the floors to scrub, the wood to chop and the potatoes to peel. And don't think you'll be playin' on the games console cos I smashed the innards out years ago." Mike tried desperately to escape round her, but she leaned forward, trapping him against the side of the lamp. His stomach finally gave way as the horror cackled manically, showing her black, ruined teeth, and ran a cold, slimy finger across his chin and down his neck.

And as her hand slithered slowly south, and Mike's knees buckled in fear, he heard her foul breath whisper, "And if h'aresole 'arry offered to swop you back one day, forget it; 'e's sitting on a beach somewhere 'ot and sunny, and 'e's gone for h'ever. Me and you 'ave got all the time in the world to get to know each other *real good*."

Oh Lucky Man!

Liam Crossman knew that most people thought he was a lucky man. What he did not know is oh how wrong most people can be!

To be fair, Liam thought he was lucky too. As he told anyone who'd listen, "I spent forty good years working in the City and managed to get out before the younger ones screwed it all up. Then I found this nice little number at my local supermarket, stocking the shelves, and chatting with the girls on the tills. After so long in the fast lane, what more could a man want!"

This night, the Manager had asked him to do an extra shift. So here he was, at half past midnight, stacking tins of 'Taste of Devon' Hog's Back Soup, and trying to think up an amusing pig rap to tell his grandchildren. It was wet and howling outside, warm and peaceful inside. Liam loved the order a well-stacked shelf represented; everything in its proper place, sitting there minding its own business. He stepped back to admire his work, and in doing so knocked a tin of baked beans off the shelf behind him. He picked it up and was about to put it back when a strange, high-pitched voice said, "Hello, my name's Heinz. What's yours?" It was odd; the voice seemed to be coming from the tin.

Liam spun round on his heel, annoyed; someone was playing a joke, throwing their voice to make it seem as if the tin was talking. But the Manager had told him he would be on his own this shift, and the night cleaner wasn't due for a couple of hours. "Who's that?" he shouted crossly, "come on, you shouldn't be in here."

"There's no one there," said the voice. "It's me, the tin. And let me ask you again, whom do I have the honour of addressing? It's very rude of you not to tell me your name."

Liam searched the shop thoroughly. He walked up and down the aisles; he checked the storeroom at the back; he went into the Manager's office, and viewed the CCTV tapes – but apart from him the shop was empty. Finally, he sat down at the Manager's desk and studied the tin carefully. "OK," he muttered to himself, "this is weird. I'm the only one in here tonight, and yet a tin of baked beans appears to be talking to me. Come on, Liam, what's going on?"

The voice spoke again, more sharply this time. "Ah, at last, a name! Well, Liam, it's not difficult. I *am* a baked beans tin, and I *am* talking to you."

If this was a trick it was a very clever one; Liam could feel the tin vibrating when it 'spoke'. He realised that if he was ever to catch the culprit he'd have to go along with things for a while. He put the tin down on the desk. "All right; let's say, just for argument's sake, that you are… what you say you are… and that your name really is Heinz. How the hell… actually, no, don't answer that, I won't understand." Liam put his hand to his forehead. "And I can't believe I'm going to ask this. Are you the only tin that talks?"

"No, most of the tins can." The tin chuckled. "Tin can; get it? That's a good one don't you think? I must tell the others."

But Liam was not amused. "Do these others have names too?"

"Yes, and it's very odd; most of them are called Heinz as well."

A sudden squall of rain rattled the shop windows, and

the wind moaned through the building's old chimneys. Liam was trying desperately not to believe what was - apparently - happening. He kept glancing through into the shop, hoping to catch sight of the trickster, but there was no one. Eventually, the tin said, "Look, Liam, it's time I told you the truth about what's happening."

"You're damn right it is!"

"There are two million of us."

"Two million of us what?"

"Talking tins of baked beans. Or is that tins of talking baked beans? I'm never quite sure, your language is so very primitive. Anyway, we're what you humans call alien invaders."

"What!" giggled Liam, "two million talking tins of baked beans are invading Earth?"

"No, now you're being silly. We're multi-dimensional, transient-form, hyperspace marauders."

"Huh?"

"We're intergalactic shape-shifters! We've disguised ourselves as tins of baked beans in order to sneak under your planet's defence. We're like your SAS, hiding in shops everywhere. Most things in this shop are shape-shifting aliens of some sort. Every planet we conquer has to supply a quota of foot soldiers. We've taught them all how to shape-shift."

"So are they disguised as tins too?!"

"Goodness me, no. Only the one pure race is allowed to be a tin. Lesser beings must disguise themselves as vegetables – Italian tomatoes, French beans, Brussel sprouts; you get the picture."

Liam put his head in his hands and groaned loudly.

"No! I don't believe a word of it. I'm hallucinating." Then he looked up as a thought occurred to him. "And anyway, why would real alien invaders break their cover, and talk to me?"

"That's a very good question, Liam. We needed to communicate with a human to understand your species better. Your radio and TV transmissions don't suggest an advanced civilisation. I mean, The Jeremy Kyle Show??"

Liam didn't know whether to be scared or flattered. "You needed to talk to *me*?"

"Not you personally. We wanted to talk to someone ordinary; nondescript. To see how they would react to a new threat. How quickly they would come to terms with it, work out counter strategies, that sort of thing. By chance we chose you."

"And?"

"It's served its purpose. I can report back that the average human is stupid, weak-minded, and incapable of high-level thought processes, but—"

"All right!" interrupted Liam. "I get the message."

"...but that you'll make good foot soldiers. Stupid always does."

Liam laughed hysterically, the absurdity of it all getting to him at last. "You're asking me to believe...? No, I'm sick; I shouldn't have eaten those mushrooms on toast."

"Ah yes," said the tin, "...about the mushrooms..."

"Don't tell me," gulped Liam, "they're shape-shifting aliens too, and I've had some of your Special Forces for my supper."

"Not quite. We've transmuted all your planet's edible

mushrooms into the poisonous variety, suitably disguised. They're on sale in all good supermarkets. Brilliant, isn't it?"

Liam sat for a while, crying quietly. He leaned forward and banged his head on the desk, trying to knock some sense into himself. And slowly, through the fog of madness, the last thread of his sanity told him he was in terrible danger. He jumped up and made a dash for the emergency exit, but as he ran down the aisle he slipped on something red and slimy and fell heavily. Scrambling up, he saw that some tomatoes had jumped out in front of him, and turned to a slippery mush as he trod on them.

Another squall hammered its drum roll of rain, louder and louder until suddenly, at its climax and as quickly as it had begun, it was gone. In the awful silence that followed, the whole shop seemed to hold its breath; waiting, expecting. Liam heard the baked beans tin bounce onto the floor, roll out of the Manager's office, and stop behind him. He turned to face it, knowing the moment of crisis had come.

"That wasn't very clever was it, Liam?" There was a quiet steeliness to the tin's voice that Liam hadn't heard before. "I was never going to let you get away." The tin sighed. "I'm afraid I'm going to have to kill you; to stop you revealing our presence. But you knew that, didn't you?"

"Do you really think anyone is going to believe me!" screeched Liam. "Hey, world, watch out for those two million talking tins of baked beans, and all those pesky fresh vegetables, they're actually shape-shifting alien invaders!"

"Sorry," said the tin, "I can't take the risk." A laser

pulse shot out from the top of the tin and blasted a hole right through Liam's stomach. "It's nothing personal you understand. I quite like you, actually."

Liam sank to his knees, staring in horror as the blood and gore splattered out over the floor, and mixed with the tomato slime. As his mind faded, the terrible truth dawned on him at last – he wasn't hallucinating, he really wasn't! "But why me?" he gasped, "why did it have to be me?"

"Just your bad luck I guess, Liam, just your bad luck. The wrong place at the wrong time." Another laser pulse blew Liam's head off.

****

The next morning, the staff arrived to find the supermarket in a terrible mess, and the shelves only half restocked. Soon after, Liam's wife reported him missing. When they discovered that the pretty young night cleaner was missing too, most people thought - well, you can imagine what most people thought. 'Oh Lucky Man!' they thought. Nobody noticed that the meat freezer was fuller than usual.

Two days later, people around the world started dying from mushroom poisoning, and the alien invasion began.

Old Myxo

"Ish it my imaginashion," slurred Penny Pound, swaying slowly back from the 'Ladies' to the bar, "or are there lotch more bleeding rabbitsh round thish year?"

"Too right," said Tuppence Tanner, the pub landlady. "They're everywhere."

Penny slid unsteadily back onto her stool. "Bit like the immigrantsh."

"They need another dose of myxomatosis."

"The immigrantsh? Harsh. I know I'm predjjj… predjudish… but—"

"No! The rabbits!"

"Ah, yesh. They've wrecked the grash on my piggery. They've even dug up the floor in thoshe old outbuildingsh I use for shtorage." Penny burped loudly and waved her empty glass at Tuppence. "It was good shtuff, that old myxo; shorted the bleedersh out. Apparentchly, there's a new shtrain appeared… aboutsh time." How Penny would soon regret her cruel words!

"The children I showed round the cellar this morning were laughing about them," said Tuppence, pouring Penny another scotch. "They love the 'bunnies'."

"Schoot the bleeding lotch of 'em."

"The children?!"

"The rabbitsh! Glad I've never had any."

"Rabbits?"

"Children!"

"Well there's still time, Penn. You're a fine-looking woman; the right man is out there somewhere."

"Thash's kind," giggled Penny, "but I'm notch really bothered." She emptied her glass in one go. "When I fed the pigsh thish morning, there were thoushands of them all over the field."

"Men?"

"Rabbitsh!"

"Of course."

"I'll have one for the road, pleash, Tuppy. Better make itsh a double."

But Tuppence hesitated. "Are you sure, Penn, you've had an awful lot. Maybe best to leave it at that."

Penny eased herself up off her stool. "I guessh show. Gottcha be out early in the morning."

"Poor you. Take care across the green, I've heard there's been some strange goings-on up there."

"Bleeding immigrantsh. Shhhould never have let them in."

"No," laughed Tuppence. "Pigs perhaps."

"Shilly woman." Penny kissed Tuppence clumsily on the cheek. "Nighcht, love."

"Night, Penn," sighed Tuppence, touching the kiss.

The cold air outside made Penny's head spin even more. She staggered and swerved up the street, every so often muttering, "Schoot the bleeding lotch of 'em." She took the gate onto the village green, but halfway across was stopped by a bright, fuzzy light on the ground in front of her. "Whatsh thish then, Pixiesh?" She stumbled to one side, but the light followed her. She bent down to look at it more closely, and slowly the one became two; a huge pair of eyes, glinting in the moonlight. "Jeezsh, a rabbitsh. A big bashtard too." Penny kicked out at it but missed wildly. Her drunken momentum lifted her other leg off the ground and she fell back, catching her head a stunning blow on a tree root.

It was several minutes before Penny stirred. Gingerly, she sat up and fingered the lump on the back of her head, which was still oozing blood. She felt woozy and light-headed. "What was that all about?!" she groaned.

"I must say, Penny Pound," said a thin, high pitched voice, "you're a better pig farmer than you are a footballer." The voice swooped and faded eerily, like an old, badly tuned radio.

"Who the...?" gasped Penny, struggling to her feet and blinking round the green.

"I'm over here."

Penny rubbed her eyes hard to try and clear the haze from them. The world seemed to swim and swirl around her, not quite in focus. "All I can see is a bleeding rabbit."

"That's me. I'm the one talking to you. Not actually talking, of course, it's more subtle than that."

"It's more nonsense, that's for sure. Come on, where are you?"

"I need to speak to you urgently," pleaded the voice. "My name is... you can call me Lewis."

"Ha," sneered Penny into the night, "and I suppose your wife's name is Carol."

"No, why? ...oh, very droll. Penny, we need your help."

"Who does?"

"For goodness sake, sit down!" Shocked by the voice's angry tone, and against her will, Penny found herself doing so. She watched in a daze as the rabbit hopped up to her. "Listen; it's me, Lewis. Do I have your attention now?" Penny nodded uncertainly. "Good. It's important I tell you this; the rabbits in my warren are dying."

"Why do I care?" sneered Penny.

"Why? Because behind all the drunken unpleasantness you're a decent person. Penny, we're in pain, our children are in pain... if you would just let me show you."

"No!" shouted Penny angrily. "Leave me alone."

Lewis shook himself. "Why do you hate us?"

"Because there's too many of you!" snorted Penny in exasperation. "You're forever trying to sneak onto my fields and take my grass and vegies. It's *my* land; I don't want you on it." She shooed him away. "Go somewhere else!"

"I see," said Lewis. "Well if that's your attitude, you'd better come with me."

Penny couldn't resist the control Lewis had over her and followed him meekly across the green and up into the woods. Towards the top of the hill, where the trees began to thin out, she glimpsed over the way the glittering of the river that bordered her farm. "We're here," said Lewis suddenly, jumping in behind a bush. Penny found him standing beside a hole set in a bank amongst the exposed roots of an old tree. "This is the main entrance to our warren. Follow me in."

"What? You want me to go down there? It's no wider than my arm; I'm not Alice in bleeding Wonderland."

"Don't be frightened. You'll find there's room enough for you to squeeze through. Come on!"

Now that Lewis was inside the warren, his hold on

Penny wasn't so strong. Nevertheless, something he'd said earlier - she wasn't even sure what - nagged at the back of her mind. She took a deep breath and crouched down. Surprisingly, she found that the hole was big enough for her to get through. "What *am* I doing?" she whispered to herself as she crawled in. "I surely must be concussed or drunk... cos I'd never do this sane or bleeding sober!"

"Welcome to my home," said Lewis with a bitter irony. "As you can see, a Wonderland it is not." Penny squatted up and looked around. The warren was dome-shaped; a little higher than her in the centre; warm and musty with a foul, sweet-sickly smell; lit by moonlight flickering eerily through tiny gaps amongst the tree roots in the roof. Spiralling up around the sides climbed a walkway, and running off this were many smaller tunnels. "Those are our living runs," explained Lewis. He saw Penny pinching her nose in distaste. "You can smell it, can you? That's all we have left in our lives, the smell of death."

"Old myxo," Penny muttered.

"What?"

Penny sat down on the walkway and rubbed her face wearily. "I said, 'old myxo'. It's what I call myxomatosis. I've smelt it many times."

"It's a new strain; it will kill us all unless we leave."

"Why don't you?"

"Because we've nowhere to go. You don't want us; your neighbours don't. You've all put up high fences."

Penny shrugged. "We need to limit the numbers of you coming in."

Lewis hopped up beside her. "Penny, whatever you think of us, I'm begging you to help our children. We call them the lost generation; they've known nothing but suffering and death. There's no future for them here; no hope. Only more death. That's why so many of them have already risked their lives to swim the river and climb your fences to migrate onto your land. They say to us, *"So what if we drown? So what if we get caught on the wire, or she shoots or traps us? We'll sure as hell die if we stay.*" Lewis sighed heavily. "It's hard to argue with them."

Penny shook her head. "There's noth—"

"But there is!" interrupted Lewis. "Take down your fences. Help them build a new life for themselves. Let them share your food, and enjoy your peace; you've got plenty." Lewis jumped onto Penny's lap and stretched up, his front feet on her chest. "Please, give the children hope."

"Get off!" shouted Penny, pushing him away. "I've told you before, it's *my* land. You're just bleeding immi…" she waved her arms, angry and confused. "…I mean rabbits."

But Lewis would not be put off. "*Just* rabbits?" he shouted back. "Is that so. And what arrogance makes you humans think you're better than us? You're not! In this world, *every* life is precious!" He banged his foot on the ground, and rabbits began to emerge from their living runs. Slowly, nervously, they hopped down the walkway and gathered in front of Penny. Many of them were mewing and crying in pain; thin and covered in oozing scabs; shivering with fever. Their faces were swollen; their lips, eyes, and ears seeped a terrible mix of pus and blood. The older ones dripped faeces and blood from their anuses. "Look at them, Penny," hissed Lewis. "Do you care for someone? Maybe there's someone you love. How would you feel if they were suffering like this?

Wouldn't you do everything you could to help them?"

Penny stared in horror at the dreadful sight. The warren loomed and swirled around her, as if to trap her in this diseased hell. Far away, she could hear Lewis begging, over and over, "Help them, Penny Pound, help the children. Take down your fences. Don't turn them away!" Overwhelmed, Penny jumped up, banging the back of her head again, and stumbled towards the entrance hole; scattering the screaming rabbits as she escaped from that terrible place. Lewis's pleading words, *"help the children, Penny, don't turn them away"*, echoed round her as she ran crying and whimpering down the hill, blundering into trees, tripping over roots, and tearing her clothes and her flesh on the bushes. As she staggered out onto the green, she stopped to retch, again and again, spitting out the vile taste of 'old myxo'. She sank to the ground; blood and tears dripping from her chin to mix with her foul vomit. "I never… realised…" she sobbed, "the children… such fear… such suffering…" She slumped forward into her mess.

For a long time, Penny was still. Eventually, as her breathing calmed and her wits returned, she managed to sit up. Her mind was clearer now, and, looking around, she found she was back where she'd originally tripped over. She stood up carefully and set off towards the village to find help. The pub was in darkness, but she banged on the door until a window opened. "Tuppy," she screamed, "it's me! Let me in!"

Tuppence ran downstairs and opened the door. "For heaven's sake," she gasped as she helped Penny into a chair, "look at the state of you! Shall I call an ambulance? The police?"

Penny raised a hand. "No, I'll be all right. I just need

to rest for a while."

"I knew something would happen to you one day," Tuppence scolded, "you drink and swear far too much. Someone was bound to take offence eventually." She knelt beside Penny. "Who was it?"

"I'm not sure," mumbled Penny. "It's like a bad dream running round in my head. Maybe it'll become clearer in a minute. I think I banged my… oh Tuppy," she started to cry, "it was blee… sorry… horrible!"

Tuppence gently stroked the tears away. "There, there," she whispered, "it's all right. Don't worry, you're with me; you're safe."

Penny smiled gratefully and took Tuppence's hand. "There is one thing I do remember. When this… whatever… was happening, all I kept thinking of was you; of how much you mean to me. Tuppy, I can't lose you." She kissed Tuppence's fingers. "I love you."

Tuppence stared at Penny for a long time and then sighed deeply. "Oh Penn. I'd always hoped, but…" Suddenly they were laughing and hugging each other as if they would never part. When they finally did, Tuppence giggled, "Wow you stink! My goodness; Penny and Tuppence an item. Hey, we could call ourselves Thrupence!"

After much more giggling, Penny said, "I also realised how selfish I've been. I've got so much; you, all that land, and my pigs. What more do I need? I'm so lucky." She went quiet for a while, her eyes far away, then whispered, "Someone said to me, somewhere, *"In this world, every life is precious."*

Tuppence play-smacked Penny's hand. "Penn, you're rambling. Who did? Where?"

Penny shrugged. "All I know is that I want, I need, to be a better person; to share my luck with others. Am I making sense?"

"Not really!"

"Tuppy, I know I moan a lot, but really I live such a comfortable life here; we all do. And there are so many people in the world, children particularly, who are suffering terribly. They're desperate to escape to a new start in life somewhere else; somewhere safe. I'd like to, I don't know, help them. Perhaps I could convert those outbuildings into accommodation for them, and let them grow crops on the top field. Something like that, anyway. Do you understand now?"

"I think so, Penn."

Penny grinned. "Good. And then there's those rabbits."

Moment of Truth

I'm standing in a small, sun-lit clearing, next to the man who shot me dead while I was sunbathing on the beach and then blew himself up.

He believes he will enter Paradise for what he did, and that I will be cast into Hell. I believe the opposite.

We worship the same God, so we can't both be right. Through the trees, we can see Him approaching. Our moment of truth.

"Good afternoon, Mr Broadhurst," smiled the School Principal coldly, ushering Ray into her office. "Sit down, please. LeftSpeak applies at this establishment."

Ray looked round nervously at the soaring hammer-beam ceiling, richly coloured wall tapestries, and great carved-oak desk - all designed to intimidate visitors. He realised this was going to be a difficult conversation. "Thank you. I came as qui—"

"Do you know why I summoned you?" interrupted the Principal.

"Oh… because you think Zac has been naughty?"

"There's no 'think' about it, Mr Broadhurst. Mrs Warner-Right reported that your son wouldn't stop talking to someone else when she spoke to him in class yesterday."

Ray shuffled uncomfortably. "Yes… he mentioned it last night. He said he couldn't help it, he was already talking to Mrs Warner's other head; Mrs Warner-Left, I believe she's called. It's hard for Zac sometimes, only having one head."

"Maybe, but we can't have him ignoring Mrs Warner-Right, can we?"

"What's he supposed to do?"

"Learn to have two conversations at the same time. Everyone else in the class can."

"Everyone else has two heads!"

"Exactly. Zac is the odd one out. Why should we make an exception for him?"

"Because he needs your help. At home, when my Left

speaks to him my Right doesn't." Ray looked the Principal in all four eyes. "Mrs Warner should do the same."

The Principal harrumphed in disagreement. "Perhaps we should talk about Zac's other... um... issue."

"What issue?"

"Him only having two arms and two legs. It's particularly noticeable at games time."

"That's because all the other children have three! I must say, Madam Principal, I'm surprised by this unpleasant monoism you're displaying. You of all people should understand that we must respect Zac's differences, not discriminate against him."

"Why should I 'understand'?" snapped the Principal. "All schools in the Imperium endorse monoism. Too many mono-head defects have been born, and we must ensure they follow our rules and customs."

"For goodness sake," shouted both Ray's heads, "Zac is not a defect! He's just different."

"Please calm down, Mr Broadhurst, and keep to LeftSpeak. It is not normal when a bi-headed foetus divides at four months, and one part is born dead. And although the other part survives, it seriously lacks in the... err... head and limb department... like Zac." The Principal wagged all three digit fingers at Ray. "He's defective."

Ray breathed deeply through both mouths, trying to keep calm. "I'm sorry, Madam Principal, but I disagree. Have you read the paper that Professor Rhys French published in the Scientifia recently?" The Principal shrugged not. "Well, his Left proposes that these are not birth defects at all, but natural adaptions. Each mono-head is slightly different from all the others. The Professor thinks humans are evolving."

"That's absurd."

"Is it? There's no doubt that in the last two million years humans have stagnated. We never do anything that's new, or difficult, or exciting. We live exactly the same lives our ancestors did ten thousand generations ago. What's the point of us? I agree with Professor French; nature wants change, and step by step it's achieving it. Zac is one of those steps."

The Principal shuffled uncomfortably. "You seem very certain about all this."

"I am; both my heads are."

Ray's Right nodded in agreement. "It took many months, but Left persuaded me."

There was a long pause as the Principal looked at Ray thoughtfully. Then she said, "You're a very unusual man, Mr Broadhurst, being able to agree with yourself. But you haven't explained what caused this so-called stagnation."

Both Ray's heads smiled. "Your own reactions show it. Your Left thinks I might have a point, your Right doesn't. It will take you years to reach a joint opinion, if ever. Most people's Left and Right rarely agree on anything even with themselves, let alone with anyone else. So nothing can ever change."

"What's wrong with things staying the same? Why do humans have to change?"

"Because our world is... the universe is... constantly; and to survive long-term humans must."

"And you think for that one head is better than two?"

"Yes, look at the evidence. Zac and his like are readily adapting to what must for them be a very alien world. Bi-heads couldn't do that."

The Principal stood up and walked slowly round her office. She hadn't been entirely truthful with Ray. She had heard of Professor French's theory, and her Left had wondered. She stopped in front of a huge plaque on the wall, listing the school's Principals over thousands of years; each one dedicated to upholding its never changing ways. She sighed; whatever some part of her might think, those names told her what she must do. She turned to Ray. "This is all very well and maybe, but I cannot make allowances for Zac's defects... differences... or help him prepare for some hypothetical ever-changing future. It's my responsibility to ensure he lives by our rules and customs. She pointed to the plaque. "As our school motto says: **'Ours Is The Only Way. It Ever Was, And Ever Must Be'**."

Ray jumped up angrily. "You've not understood a word I've said, have you?" he yelled. "That future has started, and Zac is part of it. Twenty-eight mono-heads have been born so far, and it won't be long before nature perfects them. Perhaps the next one will be the final step!" He kicked over his chair and stormed out of the office.

The Principal's heads stared after him, deep in their very different thoughts. Her Right was scornful, but her Left felt relieved, elated, by his parting words. She opened her desk drawer and took out the photoscan she had taken that morning. Her own tiny, mono-headed foetus; barely six weeks old. Right bobbled furiously, but Left smiled. "Such a beautiful baby girl," it whispered, "and, it seems, as perfect as nature intends. The mother of the future." The Principal looked up and watched Ray striding across the playground. "My Left and Right do agree on one thing, Mr Broadhurst. Twenty-nine will be the final step."

For Ever This Moment

As usual, the coach left Victoria Bus Station on time. Simon had arrived early, and managed to get his favourite seat; upstairs at the front, where other people would be the least bother. Thankfully, no one had sat next to him. He'd made this journey many times before without incident, and was not to know that today's would be very different!

It was a beautiful summer's day. As the coach drove along Buckingham Palace Road, Simon relaxed, put his jacket on the empty seat next to him, and spread himself about. But then he heard the dreaded sound - someone huffing and phewing up the aisle. His heart sank. Sure enough, a few moments later an out-of-breath woman, all hot fluster and bags, plonked herself down beside him. "Gosh, that was close," she gasped. "This is the coach to Leicester, isn't it? I was in such a rush."

"It is," Simon said tersely. "And I don't wish to be rude, but you're sitting on my jacket."

"Oops, I'm so sorry." The woman stood up and brushed it down. "Shall I put it on the luggage rack for you? And while I'm up, I'll put my things on here too." With more huffing and phewing, and leaning over and generally getting in Simon's face, she did. As she sat down again, she said, "My name's Hannah, by the way."

"Simon." He glanced at her quickly, in that way quiet people do in such situations. He got the impression of a middle-aged, slightly overweight woman; not unattractive.

"Why are you off to Leicester today, Simon?"

Simon sighed, resigned to talking. "I'm... um..." he

paused; for some reason, his mind had gone blank. To hide his confusion, he waved at the open laptop on his knees, and said, "Look, I'm sorry, I've got a lot of work to do."

"Of course, forgive me. I've got something to do too." Hannah pulled a notepad and pencil out of her handbag and started writing. But after a while, she looked over at Simon's laptop, and said, "Sorry again, and I know I'm being nosey; what are you writing?"

"Oh, it's nothing really," said Simon sheepishly. "Just a science fiction short story about a teenager who runs away from a broken home, and joins a space mission to explore Mars."

"My goodness," exclaimed Hannah.

"That's very kind of you, but I'm afraid the plot's not exactly original."

"No, that's not what I meant. I'm writing a short story too. I'm an English teacher, and I've asked my sixth form pupils for a two-thousand-word piece of fiction. I thought I'd better have one of my own ready for them."

"What a coincidence," smiled Simon. "I retired recently from the Merchant Navy; went round the world nine times. I read a lot of science fiction on my rest days, most of it very bad, so I thought I'd have a go at writing something myself."

"Well then," laughed Hannah, "happy scribbling to both of us."

For the next twenty minutes, Simon sat silent writing his story. As was his way, he thought about things, wrote something down, scratched his nose, made some deletions, and wrote some more. He noticed that Hannah was more ordered with her story; thinking for longer, and seemingly happy with what she wrote first time. But, as they joined the motorway, she muttered, "No, no, this isn't right," reversed her pencil, and started rubbing out furiously.

At the same moment, Simon felt a violent pain in his right foot. "Ouch," he yelped, and reached down to massage it - *but it wasn't there*! Then he felt the same pain in his left foot. "What the hell..." He pulled his legs up in front of him, only to find that both his feet had disappeared. He watched in horror as his legs started to fade away too. "What's happening to me?" he screamed.

Hannah looked up. "My God, what's going on?"

"I don't know. When you started rubbing out your story I started to disappear!"

"Don't be silly. Look..." Hannah rubbed out some more - Simon's knees faded. "Goodness, you're right. What on earth?" She put her hand to her mouth. "Heavens, surely not, how can that be? Simon, I think I know what's happening; you must be him, the man."

"What are you talking about? What man?"

"The man in my story. He's on a coach journey too. When I started to rub him out, you started to, I don't know... not exist." Hannah gasped. "Hey, but that means you're not real; that you only exist because I'm writing about you."

"That's rubbish. I'm me, I'm Simon Carter."

"Is it rubbish? Where do you live?"

Again, Simon's mind went blank. "I... err... hell, I can't remember."

"How did you get to the bus station?"

"...I've no idea."

"And you couldn't remember why you're going to Leicester, could you?" Simon was silent. "You see. That's because I haven't written those bits of my story yet."

Simon shook his head. "No, no, I don't believe you. I've caught this coach before, I know I have. And I remember being in the Merchant Navy."

"So does my character. You have those memories because I wrote them."

"Oh, come on, that doesn't make sense. I've had those memories for years, and you didn't know about them until we met today." Simon slapped Hannah's notebook angrily. "You only started writing them down after that. The timeline isn't right."

Hannah put her hand on his arm to calm him. "Isn't that the point about a short story? Anything can happen, including time being twisted inside out all wrong. A moment can last for ever, or vice versa. Time can be whatever we want it to be."

"But what about the other people on this coach?" asked Simon, still confused. "How come they exist? You haven't written about them, have you? I know I haven't."

"No." Hannah glanced behind them, and then back at Simon. "See for yourself."

Simon turned round, but instead of the expected coachload of travellers, all he could see was a grey, swirling confusion of... nothingness; an absence of anything. "I don't understand, where are they?"

"Now take a look outside."

Simon peered through the panoramic window in front of them. There was the motorway he knew so well, disappearing away ahead of the coach. "And?"

"Keep looking," said Hannah quietly." Tell me what

you can actually see."

After a while, Simon realised something was wrong, something he'd never noticed before - there was no other traffic. No cars, no lorries; nothing. And on either side of the motorway was that grey, swirling emptiness. Slowly, he turned and stared open-mouthed at Hannah.

"That's right," she nodded. "Apart from mentioning the motorway briefly, and the nice weather, I haven't written anything about what's outside the coach; as far as my character is concerned there's no such place."

"All right," groaned Simon, "one final test. Rub out some more of your story." Hannah did so, and his left hand faded away.

There was a long silence as the terrible truth began to sink in. Eventually, Simon mumbled, "I don't exist, do I? I'm a figment of your imagination."

"You do exist, you're in my story."

"Are all my memories and thoughts yours?"

"Your memories are. But I haven't written anything for several minutes, so you're probably having your own thoughts now."

"What..." Then Simon paused, an extraordinary idea growing. "Wait a minute, if I'm only a..." He pressed the 'Backspace' button on his laptop. This time it was Hannah who screamed - now *her* feet were fading away. "There," shouted Simon, "I knew it. If I'm just a character in a story then the only way you can exist to me is if you're a story character as well. You're disappearing, so you must be the woman I'm deleting." Simon held his finger down on 'Backspace', and Hannah's legs started to disappear.

"What are you doing?" she yelled.

"I'm deleting all of you. Maybe then this nightmare will end, and I'll get my legs back."

"No, stop. *Stop!*" Hannah reached over and pushed Simon's hand away from his laptop. "Don't you see? If you delete me, my story will cease to exist too; and so will you, because that's the only place where you... are. Gosh, this is complicated." She giggled. "You know, I wasn't going to rub out my title." She showed Simon the front of her notepad; it read 'Race to the Bottom'. "That's all there would have been left of you."

But Simon was not in the mood for humour. "So, we're saying that we're characters in each other's stories and that the only way we'll survive is if neither of us deletes the other from them."

"It would seem so."

"Does the opposite apply? That if we don't delete each other we'll live for ever?"

"Simon! One minute you're asking me if you exist, now you're asking if you're eternal. What do I know? I guess it depends if the stories we write are eternal."

Simon took a slow, deep breath. "OK, try this; is there anything else except our stories?"

"What do you mean?"

Simon pointed out of the window at the empty greyness. "Are you and I... our stories... all there is? Or are there other characters, other stories, out there somewhere in all that?"

Hannah shrugged. "Now you mention it, it does seem odd I know about things like Leicester and the Merchant Navy. I wonder if they exist in another story, which is somehow leaking into ours." She sighed. "Or maybe I made them up. Anyway, I think we should write each other back into our stories properly; make us whole again." She looked Simon up and down quizzically. "And I could make some improvements while I'm at it."

"Good idea," harrumphed Simon.

Simon and Hannah redrafted their stories, and slowly their legs and feet returned. Eventually, Simon stopped typing, and said, "Done it."

"Me too," said Hannah. She looked Simon over. "Mm, not bad. Here, take a look at the rewritten 'you'." She took a small mirror out of her handbag.

"Hey, I look like Johnny Depp."

"You wouldn't believe what he and I get up to in my dreams. Last night, we..." Hannah stopped as Simon grinned at her. "What? Oh, I see, you wrote those dreams." She smacked his arm. "You're a naughty man. Give me the mirror." She looked at herself and burst out laughing. "Madonna?"

"When I was a teenager, I had rude posters of her all over my bedroom walls. At night, I used to shine a torch on them, and—"

"Please, enough." interrupted Hannah, "I know!"

Simon blushed. "Who's the naughty one now?" When he'd recovered his composure, he said, "All right, what happens next? What are the next chapters in our stories... our lives?"

Hannah looked coy. "Well, seeing as we've created sexual fantasies of each other, I think we should write about a hotel bedroom, and see what happens."

"That sounds like fun."

"And if we want to live for ever we'd better write ourselves a long-term affair."

"A *very* long one," laughed Simon. "We don't ever have to leave the bedroom. Imagine, never-ending sex!"

Hannah smiled. "Nice idea, but there'll surely come a time when we'll want to move our stories on."

"Then I'll rewrite you as someone else. Or maybe a threesome. Me, Madonna and Kylie; now there's a thought and a half."

"Who's Kylie?"

"Um… good question. But I like the idea of her!"

"Stop it, I'm being serious."

"All right. Actually, I've written that I'm in love with you, and always will be whoever you are."

"Why Simon, that's so sweet." Hannah scribbled on her notepad. "There, now I'm in love with you too. I suppose if we're right about all this, you're the first man I've ever fallen for."

"If we're right about all this, I'm the first man you've ever met!"

They laughed, happy just to be with each other in all this confusion, and Hannah snuggled into Simon's shoulder. "But after your fantasy threesome, *then* what do we do with our stories? We can write anything we want."

"And we've got all the time there is to do it - assuming unwritten stories are eternal too."

Hannah glanced up at Simon, a strange look in her eyes. "Do you think they are?"

"As you said, my love, what do I know?" Simon scratched his nose. "One thing is certain, though, it will take a lot of thought."

The coach journeyed on through the grey, swirling

eternity of stories written and unwritten. Upstairs, Simon sat hand in hand with Hannah, wondering about their future together. It wasn't clear to him any more quite who was thinking what, or writing what, about whom, and it didn't much matter. He knew they were bound together for ever, each not able to exist without the other, living lives limited only by their imaginations. He leant over and kissed Hannah. "Maybe we should go looking for those other stories, see if they exist, and write their characters into ours."

Hannah sighed deeply. "Maybe, but..."

"...But?"

"...I've been thinking. I've never written a story much longer than two thousand words. I don't..." Hannah paused, choosing her words carefully. "I don't want to turn our lovely short stories into horrible long ones."

Simon looked at her thoughtfully. "So?"

Hannah stroked his cheek, his eyes, his lips. "So why don't we stop writing? Finish our stories right here, right now; with you and me the only characters in them, just living in *this* moment." She put her notepad and pencil back in her bag. "For ever."

They kissed again for a long time. "That gets my vote," whispered Simon. He pressed 'Save' on his story file, and closed the laptop.

Available worldwide from

Amazon

---

www.mtp.agency

www.facebook.com/mtp.agency

@mtp_agency

Printed in Great Britain
by Amazon